The Going Down

Duncan Barford

The Going Down

Duncan Barford

SPHINX

ISBN (perfect): 978-19159-523-8-7
ISBN (epub):978-19159-523-9-4

First printed April, 2025
by Sphinx
(an imprint of Sul Books, LTD)
Lewes, UK / Rodenbourg, LUX

Cover and Interior Design: Sul Books

Find our books at SULBOOKS.COM

Molly was to me not a woman, but the thing which is woman. And because I saw not her, but what was behind her, life came in with such a rush that we were whirled away like leaves in the wind. The barriers of personality went down, and we were made one with the cosmic life — not one with each other, for that, I think, can never be, and we miss the turning when we seek it...

— Dion Fortune, *The Sea Priestess* (1938).

ephemera

It wasn't the beginning. Other circumstances had quietly fallen into place, or else he would never have noticed the pylons. As the train sped through the flat, green land, Bailey saw them. He looked up and was surrounded.

The summer was wet, and the light fading, although there should have been a good two hours left. Clouds were broiling, dark and low, and above the train's aggravated whine he heard fat raindrops pelting the windows. Slowly, he twisted in his seat. All around, striding to the distance in radiating lines, the pylons shouldered their burden of undulating cable over the murky horizon. The nearest passenger, several rows behind, was oblivious. The summer gloom, the rain, and a sense of the train traversing some mysterious nexus, these produced a feeling of imminent arrival at a hidden centre. They would slide into an unmarked, unnamed station, and he would be the only passenger alighting, and then: whatever the pylons promised would be revealed.

But the train hurtled on. The rain lashed the windows and the darkness thickened. Bailey realised the trajectory was wrong. He was moving past the mystic point from which the pylons radiated.

Already, the landscape was changing. The ranks of striding pylons receded behind him, their secrets undeciphered, as the train nuzzled the outskirts of Luton. Allotment gardens flashed past, and then suburban housing. The next stop was the city centre. The train was braking, but Bailey remarked neither the deceleration, nor the halt and beeping of the doors, nor the rain-dishevelled passengers clambering on.

Albeit beneath the same dreary weather, the pylons had seemed luminous. The train admitted no outside sound but, as they passed, it seemed to Bailey he heard the drone of high-tension wires, the fizz and crackle they make in wet air. He couldn't shake the compulsion to encroach. Suppose he went to live out there, like a contemporary hermit, meditating in a tent. He would lead a contemplative life beneath those monoliths of infrastructure. The drone and crackle of their wires a constant background chant, he would discern their sonic variations under shifting conditions of drizzle, mist, and sleet. On sunny days he'd chart the dilation of the pylons' shadows across the land. Some kind of revelation lay in store, which — if it resisted him — he'd force open.

Fits of imaginative passion were not alien to him. Something was calling out, for sure, but this might be only a feeling, displaced and triggered by what happened over the weekend.

He was returning from a visit to his closest friend. When Steve phoned, it had been evening and Bailey was drinking alone in his darkening room. He'd heard an uncharacteristic edge of panic in his friend's voice. Steve was moving out of the old house but had put off packing and clearing until the deadline had drawn uncomfortably close. Like Bailey, Steve preferred a circle of friends small in number, but close. The disadvantage, and the cause of Steve's desperation, was that at such short notice no one was free to help. But Bailey, a little resentful of being taken for granted, agreed to travel up at the weekend and assist.

"It'll give us both the chance to say goodbye properly to the house," Steve consoled him.

That was precisely what Bailey had hoped to avoid. Steve had grown up there, and Bailey grew up in a house similar, two streets away, but his parents had sold up following their separation during Bailey's first term at university. Afterwards, Steve's house became the place to which Bailey returned, the link with his childhood, and Steve, when he was a student, had attended the university closest, coming back so often he practically lived at home. Older than Bailey's parents, but still so relatively young, Steve's parents had died within months of each other, just before he turned thirty. That small, terraced house for both of them was a palace of memory.

"I can't get over that you're actually moving. You've never lived anywhere else."

"I think you'll miss it more than I will," said Steve.

Bailey's happiest time had been a couple of years after Steve had inherited the house. Bailey moved in as Steve's lodger and had stayed for the best part of a decade. If he helped Steve with the move, but made his exit before the removal van, then he could imagine Steve still living there. This was not logical, but logic — Bailey reasoned — never helped anyone cope with change.

"Fine. I'll come," he agreed at last.

"I'll make it up to you," said Steve.

By the time the call ended it was dark. Bailey took a pull on his beer. From upstairs came the sound of his landlord's television: a football match. What he'd avoided asking, and which Steve hadn't volunteered, was whether Donna would be there. So, at last, she'd got what she wanted from Steve, but Bailey doubted she'd come along to gloat. She was always unerringly polite in his company, but after several years of it, superficiality was all he'd grown to expect from her.

The years were passing quickly. What had they to show for it? Steve had a stable relationship and a steady job, and was moving into a nice, new home, while Bailey was looking back over a few strange and failed relationships, and a string of jobs that amounted not to a career, but to what suspiciously resembled an avoidance of one. Maybe it was a perverse pride he felt.

Before sliding into his unmade bed, Bailey took stock: many suppose themselves in opposition to the mainstream, he reasoned, but where this merely masks a sense of failure, then it's fake. He searched inside himself, trying to determine whether his life's course were truly chosen, not followed, and he drifted off to sleep.

He dreamed of salmon leaping against the river's flow, where, at sunset, he walked a footpath along the bank. Each fish leapt and flared iridescent in the slanted light. Eager to share the spectacle, he turned, smiling, to the woman beside him. His heart sank: she was not there, and the feeling of wonder — superseded by disappointment — lingered with him into the morning, which puzzled him, because the dream that caused it had dissolved entirely from his memory.

Donna sat on the porch step, nursing a mug of tea. She recognised Bailey the moment he rounded the corner of the street, and she braced herself for the inevitable awkwardness. He hadn't seen her, which gave her the opportunity to observe how the years seemed to sit heavier upon him than on Steve, exacerbating how he'd always looked a little too old for how he dressed: baggy jeans, and a denim jacket decorated with occult insignia which, she supposed, Steve understood but, thankfully, didn't share Bailey's need to broadcast. He then noticed her, and put up his hand, making a little grimace, an ironic placeholder for a smile, which told her plainly he hadn't expected she would be there.

"Hey," said Donna, as he drew within speaking distance. "Good to see you. How was the journey?"

"Fine," sighed Bailey. "So," he said, "Steve's given in, at last. Ready for the big move?"

There it was, as usual: the implication that Steve wasn't doing what he wanted, that it was all her connivance.

"I guess so," she said.

"Is he inside?" said Bailey.

She nodded, and, without getting up, leant sideways so he could pass.

"I'll see you in a bit, then," said Bailey, stepping over her. "Sorry."

"No problem," she said.

A moment later, she heard them shouting and slapping each other. Steve needed friends; she didn't begrudge that, and even though they weren't seeing each other as much these days, she didn't doubt that Bailey's intentions were genuine. But Bailey didn't understand how Steve was changing. In truth, maybe they all needed to change. She knew that she did, and probably so did Bailey, if for nothing else, then to make up for lost time, because they were having to do now what they should have done years ago. The amount of time it took these days to secure the basics of a decent life: it felt typical of the era they were living through.

The inside of the house had fallen quiet. The boys had gone into the garden. She smelt cleaning products, and that dank, dark smell that houses release when carpets are pulled up, and furniture is moved that has stood in the same place for years and years. From among the pile of boxes awaiting collection in the hall, she picked out the smallest, and sorted through it until she held what she was looking for. She knew Steve's parents only from this handful of photographs. It had been a while since she last perused them. There they were, Steve's mum and dad: his graduation; driving test; the three of them, posing alongside a girlfriend he had at university. Rooms in this very house formed the backdrops, recognisable but different. Steve's mum and dad had been a happy, average couple. He'd kept no photographs of them looking ill, nor any of his dad after his mum had died. Donna sighed.

Steve had come in. She hadn't noticed, and he watched her for a moment. Even from a distance he knew what she was holding, and it surprised him. She'd not looked at those for a couple of years. Today, the last day in the house where he'd grown up, he felt the presence of his parents all the more strongly. Although she'd never known them, evidently it seemed that Donna sensed them too. As he moved closer, she looked up, stood, and quietly they held each other.

"You okay?" she said.

"I'm okay. You?"

"Where's Bailey?"

"Feeding the fire. There's plenty of stuff left to burn."

"Have a good time with your friend," she said, "and come back to mine when you're done. Don't stay here on your own."

"You're sure you're okay?" he said.

She nodded, but felt sad, and — underneath, oddly, from somewhere — she was angry, too. But not at Steve. She didn't think so, anyway.

"It's taken us so long to get to this point," she said. "Things just got in the way."

She knew that Steve would know precisely what and who she meant. Before they had met, it had taken years until she realised how abusive it was, and how pointless. Years wasted, which she'd never get back. Seeing Steve's house packed and emptied was bringing back feelings from the last time she'd had to move.

Steve reached out to hold her again, and she let him.

"It'll feel different from now on," he said. "It will."

In the garden, Bailey was throwing old books and papers, and jaded knickknacks from the seventies and eighties, and all the other things charity shops refuse, into a rusted oil-drum where a vicious blaze consumed them.

"Donna's headed back," said Steve, joining him. "There's beer in the fridge."

Bailey nodded. So, this was the plan, then: him and Steve. He tossed a sheaf of ancient phone bills into the flames, recoiling as a gust sent smoke and heat back into their faces. It didn't feel right, fire on a summer's day, but a long summer evening was exactly what they'd need to put the house in order and make their farewell.

Steve noticed Bailey wasn't saying much but knew better than to ask. Direct questions would only elicit evasion and, honestly, Steve was happy to let Bailey play the role of chief mourner. It saved Steve from having to probe his own sorrows and doubts. He could feel how Bailey's anguish over the move was partly feigned. Steve knew that Bailey resented Donna, although he'd never admit it. It wasn't jealousy, but it might be envy. Bailey's own relationship status was vague: no girlfriend, but, instead, a long-term ex who, as far as Steve could tell, he still saw regularly. Steve had met her only once, and the encounter had been so strange they'd barely spoken of it since but, one day, Steve knew, they would probably need to, because he'd seen something that perhaps Bailey ought to know.

They spent the day between rooms: sorting, packing, moving, and carrying junk outside to burn. Steve, grinning, beckoned Bailey into the rear bedroom, the room that had been Bailey's when he'd lodged with Steve.

"Shit," Bailey said.

The carpet was gone and the floorboards bare. After Bailey moved in, Steve let him paint the floorboards black, but they'd both forgotten the insignia Bailey had painted on top, in white, back in the days when they'd dabbled in demonology: the circle to stand inside for safety, and, around its circumference, magical words of power in Greek, to make doubly sure.

"We'd better sort that out," said Steve, "or else the new owners will freak."

They worked on hands and knees, scrubbing with old rags drenched in white spirit. It didn't come off at all neatly, but the grey smudges they reduced it to looked far less sinister.

"Considering what happened, I can't believe you carried on sleeping in here," said Steve.

"I never believed anything lingered," smirked Bailey, "given that it never seemed to confine itself to this room anyway."

"That's true," nodded Steve.

They'd learnt how summoning demons produces appearances more complex and subtle than flesh-and-blood gremlin creatures; sometimes nothing more than an eerie feeling of being watched, or a strange smell or atmosphere — usually malevolent. Sometimes it was even more subjective, such as an intrusive thought, or the impulse to say or do something out of character. The danger of these rituals, they soon realised, were experiences impossible to distinguish from personal mental processes. The knack was to keep all possibilities open, because being too certain of one of them, or falling into confusion between them, could lead to consequences that might all too easily be labelled "mental illness," or could be described in even less reassuring terms.

The house had a weird atmosphere at times. Whenever it rained at night, they were likely to discover each other awake, too agitated to sleep. A few times, it'd been so bad they'd sat in the kitchen together, listening to the rain, trying to find words for how it felt. "As if the house were changing shape," Steve suggested, and Bailey agreed. It felt like the rain were feeding something in the house the energy it needed to grow a secret room. On those nights, it seemed there were a parallel house, invisible, alongside theirs, where something else was living.

They coped with the splashback from these experiments by never sharing the house with anyone else, but, of course, like attracts like, and often they ran across others with similar interests. In a pub one night, through mutual friends, they talked with a woman who told them she'd miscarried and that in her handbag was the foetus in a jar. She suggested they held a ritual at their house to lay its spirit to rest. Extricating themselves had been delicate. Traumatised people, finding themselves in dark places, reaching out for rescue, but dragging in to drown with them anyone offering help: Steve and Bailey knew that to offer assistance, a person had to stand on dry ground. Were these merely encounters with instances of poor mental health, or something disguising itself as that? It was safest, always, never to assume that they knew.

Demons in the back bedroom, and in the big bedroom at the front where Steve slept, they'd scried the Enochian aethyrs: thirty astral visions each, sixty in total. It'd taken them two years to complete. Downstairs, in the back room ("the dining room" as Steve's parents had called it), they'd conjured spirits from Dee and Kelley's elemental tables, and performed other, more run-of-the-mill rituals. But the lounge at the front had always been a magick-free zone, a space for grounding themselves and resting in everyday reality.

On this final day, the rooms bare, and echoing, and progressively emptier, they were shutting down the space entirely, turning off the magick. Would the new owners feel the house morphing on rainy nights? As he carried more junk downstairs for burning, it didn't seem likely to Bailey. So many spirits they'd trafficked through these rooms, beings unconstrained by an experience of time, or a sense of a difference between internal and external. Once here, perhaps a spirit always was. Maybe, Bailey ruminated, what's done is never undone. Because life ends, it's supposed that actions dissolve away. He no longer believed that. Everything thought, or done, or intended, none of it vanishes. It persists, through the miniscule effects that it continues to exert. Every spirit summoned in that house would never completely fade. Would it have been better never to have summoned anything?

Far too late, of course. Bailey and Steve had been teenagers when they crossed that bridge. They'd met in the Horror section of the town library, and then had sought each other out at school, to share their latest discoveries at breaktimes. Bailey's parents didn't mind, but Steve's tried to persuade him this interest was "silly" or "morbid." Hiding books to read secretly at night only heightened the enjoyment. The material Steve hadn't space to conceal, Bailey kept for him. Steve's parents relented as he aged, realising his attention might have been captured by far worse. They no longer frowned on Bailey's presence, nor seemed to mind what the boys were doing during all those hours up in Steve's room. What mattered was knowing where they were.

The burner in the garden accepted another donation of junk. Steve was chatting with the neighbours over the fence: an old couple, the age Steve's parents would have been. Their kids flew the nest years ago, and they were joking with Steve about how he'd, instead, come home there to roost. Bailey often wondered why Steve chose to live on at the house after his parents passed, and why he'd turned the place over to magick, because his parents wouldn't have liked that. But it's impossible to make dead people happy; it's hard enough to please the living. Had Steve's parents lived to old age, Bailey doubted they could have turned Steve into someone he didn't want to be. Yet maybe if the house hadn't become a two-man magical temple, Steve might have settled down sooner with someone like Donna. Back then, it would never have crossed Steve's mind; it was only quite recently that he'd started making other plans.

After their final goodbye to Steve, the neighbours returned indoors. "They were here before Mum and Dad moved in," he said wistfully. "They were telling me how Mum and Dad, on the day they moved in, lit a bonfire that burned all night and pissed off half the street."

"That was a bit passive-aggressive," said Bailey. "Shall we put it out?"

"I don't think they meant it like that."

Two more hours of packing and clearing, and the afternoon had slipped into evening. The light turned golden, and pizzas were delivered. They took beers and sat in the garden to eat.

"You think it's a bad idea, me moving in with Donna, don't you?"

"There's only one good reason for you to do that: because you want to."

"I do want to."

"Then it's a good idea."

"I can't be like you, Bailey."

"Why would you want to be?"

"I'm not unhappy about moving on, despite all the memories."

Bailey was quiet. He seemed to be searching for something that was difficult to express. "It's the end of our magick, and it feels like maybe it's the end of all the magick that was ever done by a couple of guys."

Steve chuckled. "It was a long and noble tradition."

"Dee and Kelley," nodded Bailey, "Crowley and Neuberg."

"Parsons and Hubbard," laughed Steve.

"I never suggested it always turned out well!"

"Actually, it seems designed not to."

"That's what I'm getting at," said Bailey. "It has a particular dynamic whose moment seems to be passing."

Steve guessed where Bailey was heading. That very same week, someone at work had told Steve that his opinions were skewed by his straight, cis, white, male privilege. He wasn't used to being shut down and talked to like that. He'd felt shocked and hurt, but it had made him think about how people less privileged than himself probably experienced that kind of thing far more often, usually from people who looked like him. It happened during the unconscious bias training his company had arranged, and the person who'd voiced it was one of the other trainees. Probably she was right: he must change his outlook. He needed to become (as she'd suggested) an ally to others in their struggle for what he'd always taken for granted.

"But," he reflected, telling Bailey the story, "if it's okay for her to shut me up, yet not vice versa, then some identities are more equal than others. So, was she possibly just acting like a dick?"

"Identitarianism has thoroughly fucked the Left," Bailey sighed.

"Neoliberal capitalism continues on its merry way," said Steve, "while we argue over who's the most oppressed."

"Fuck identity," agreed Bailey.

"Exactly what a cis, white, straight male can afford to say," said Steve.

"White?" said Bailey. "I'm beyond the fucking pale."

"I can't believe you said that," Steve groaned. "You deserve to be cancelled, after a joke like that."

"What isn't seen or heard becomes occult," Bailey said.

necromancy

The light was fading and the fire, which hadn't been fed in a while, had lost its blaze. Holes and cracks in the burner exposed the molten-red interior, traversed by almost invisible licks of flame. The pizza and beer had relaxed them. The work was almost done. The removal van would arrive tomorrow and, once it had loaded and departed, a new phase would begin for Steve, without his childhood home, without the place in which he'd discovered and explored so much of what formed him.

Fuck identity, Bailey had said.

"How about one final magical working?" said Steve.

"There's still so much stuff to sort out," Bailey sighed.

"If we start early tomorrow, there'll be time."

"What did you have in mind?"

"Ancestors," said Steve. "Those that came before and have passed down what has become who we are."

Every transition is a death in miniature, every transformation, and every change. The beginning of a new phase is a time crucial for reconnection with the dead, whether to seek their blessing, so that there can be continuity with the past, or to make an offering, strike a bargain, so that the dead may loosen any grip they have on the present, and allow a clean break.

"You're sure you want to do that here?" Bailey said.

Steve understood what he was getting at. Mum and Dad, his closest ancestors, had both died in the house and would not approve of him holding rituals there. It might be unwise to open a magical space that they could easily step through.

"Suppose you summoned the spirit of some arch atheist after they'd died," said Steve, "they'd never show up, would they? Else they'd be admitting they were wrong."

"Your logic is implacable," Bailey laughed.

"Mum and Dad won't show," insisted Steve.

This didn't seem unreasonable, but Bailey knew that it was always better in magick to rule out complications. Bailey had once extracted a promise from Steve that, if Bailey died first, Steve would never make him an object of necromantic magick. Bailey had met magicians who'd maintained magical links with dead partners or friends. It seemed presumptuous to suppose this wasn't harmful to the dead, or that their consent wasn't an issue. He couldn't control what Steve, or anyone, might do after he was dead, but he hoped it were true (as Steve seemed to be suggesting) that the dead hold a power of veto on whether to appear before the living.

"What would be our intention in doing this?" Bailey asked.

"To ask the ancestors our best way forward."

"What do they know? They were probably racist, sexist, and homophobic. How is their advice going to help us now?"

Steve had done a little research into his family tree. Since the Industrial Revolution, his forebears had spent their lives working in factories, focused mainly on avoiding destitution and trying not to get killed in wars. Before the factories, they'd worked on the land. This was probably the case for most people's ancestors.

"Perhaps they learned a thing or two about how to survive, and how to avoid being fucked over," said Steve.

They decided, for the first time ever, and the last, to perform the ritual in the lounge, the largest room at the front of the house, where everything had been cleared, apart from the curtains, which they drew closed to shield themselves from anyone passing along the street. They hauled in an old garden hose, and arranged it in a circle that extended close to the walls. This would offer a protective boundary against any malign spirits. A light bulb remained in the socket hanging overhead, casting a brownish light over the floorboards and stripped walls. The once homely room had an acoustic now of echoes and emptiness, an element of strangeness that induced a sense of skewed reality even before they'd started.

Steve retrieved his ghost box from a crate: a battery-powered transistor radio, a model long obsolete, formerly mass-produced by RadioShack, which, through considerable effort and cost, he'd sourced second-hand. This radio was vulnerable to a hack. Following directions from a video posted to a paranormal investigation forum, Steve had opened its casing and snipped off with pliers a specific component. The radio was no longer capable of locking onto a frequency; it could only cycle helplessly across the AM or FM waveband. Useless now for listening to stations, it was usable instead as the audio equivalent of a black mirror, that ancient tool of magicians and witches, helpful for obtaining visions and talking with spirits.

The ritual was Steve's idea, so Steve would lead it and Bailey would facilitate. Steve shut the door and they stood in the centre of their improvised hosepipe circle. First, they banished, executing a series of movements and chants to clear the surroundings of unwanted influences and to prime it for what followed. It was a sequence they'd performed so many times it was automatic, and therein lay the challenge of a thorough banishing: confidence balanced against sensitivity to the well-worn words and sounds, so that the meaning of their actions was clear and present to their minds; sharp, vivid, and alert.

Steve nodded at Bailey, the signal for Bailey to walk the inside perimeter of the circle, voicing an ad hoc enchantment: "Fortify this, our solid and sacred boundary, against all malign and interfering spirits ..." Bailey's words, as he traced the circle, weren't a description, nor an entreaty, but the means by which what he spoke had already become the case and was already happening.

Bailey nodded back to Steve: the circle was secure. Steve readied himself with a moment of silence before his invocation of the dead. In imagination he sensed them at the circle's outer edge, like a crowd approaching slowly through fog. He felt for the words to make it real, but if he'd already found the feeling, then it wouldn't matter much what he said. One Halloween, they'd called in the ancestors with a football chant, simply repeated over and over until the ancestors came: "Come on, you dead! Come on, you dead!" Not an eloquent incantation, but it caught the mood. It half crossed his mind to use that now, but then: "From out of the earth I call the dead," he said. "Come up from your graves, from your scattered ashes. I call to you, our ancestors, born of this land, and voyagers to this land. You, our forebears, we invite, to share this offering."

Bailey poured beer into a glass and set it on the floor.

"We welcome you," said Steve, "with respect and good will, to join us in conversation, so that we might benefit from your wisdom."

Receiving a nod from Steve, Bailey switched on the ghost box. It gave out a stuttering whisper as it cycled in rapid intervals across its waveband: fragments of music, speech, white noise, an audio collage of whatever stations were broadcasting in that instant. This random melange of sound was the medium through which what had no voice would speak, because by what means other than coincidence could they interact with what doesn't participate in causality, having no physical form.

Words from the ghost box: *opening into … twice … above …*

The atmosphere was changing, thickening, as when a storm gathers; a feeling that something, certainly, was going to happen. When the weather changes, there's a sense of presence; even in an everyday gust of wind that sets swaying the tops of the trees. Something is doing that. It is windy. It is raining. Meaning is presence, and something was speaking.

Can be found … in talks today … just before half-time …

Steve and Bailey exchanged glances. They both could feel it: the dead were about to be heard.

"We sense your presence," said Steve. "Thank you for joining us."

Eighteen minutes past … completely inadequate … [the sound of laughter from an audience] …

"We called you to this house, where I've lived since a child, because tomorrow I leave forever."

I can't imagine … which he denies …

"My life is changing, and the whole world feels like it is changing too. Can you advise us on the best way to deal with what lies ahead?"

In the space of a week … [country and western music] … fif-teen Palestinians killed … current forecast …

"Some kind of hurt or loss, in the short term?" Bailey suggested.

"What was that music?"

"I don't know. 'Stand By Your Man'? Sounded like Dolly Parton, or something."

Steve addressed the dead: "Thank you for your answer."

The ghost box continued stuttering out its fragments. Capturing all of them wasn't the point, nor was objectivity the issue, but wherever timing and attention happened to fall — that was important.

"Harm in the short term," said Steve. "Is that correct?"

Transexual athletes … really has no clue … hardness of a dia-mond … do I look bothered? …

"A struggle: difficult, because we'll approach it in a clue-less way," interpreted Bailey. "Is that right?"

The ghost box fell quiet.

Steve and Bailey looked at one another, surprised.

There was a hiss of static and, faintly, classical music from a distant-sounding station.

"It's stopped cycling," said Bailey, picking up the ghost box and pressing the button marked SCAN, but with no ef-fect. Turning the power switch off and on again made no difference.

"How?" said Steve. "I don't understand. The physical component that enables it to tune in literally isn't there."

"It must've grown back," Bailey joked.

The doorbell in the hallway chimed. They both froze and looked at one another. Steve shook his head in re-sponse to Bailey's unasked question: no, he wasn't expect-ing anyone.

"Hello?" Steve called towards the window. The doorstep to the porch was right outside. Whoever was there would hear him. But there was no response.

Neither was naive enough to imagine leaving the circle to answer the door. Stepping outside would forgo their protection. The most common way for spirits to lure a magician was to pretend the ritual hadn't worked, and the second was what perhaps they were facing now: a decoy or distraction. If someone were really on the doorstep, then why hadn't they answered Steve? In the long silence that followed, no footfalls were heard receding and, as they listened and waited, it felt as if something were listening and waiting too.

"Can you feel that?" said Steve.

Bailey could, but he hadn't wanted to say so, because that might influence Steve's perception, and besides, if Steve hadn't put it into words, there seemed no benefit from drawing attention to something that felt so bad and was growing steadily worse.

From the ghost box: only the distant piano concerto, obscured by static. The locus of communication had shifted to the silence on the doorstep and the atmosphere in the room, a palpable and expanding cloud of emotion, as when, in a family situation, or at work, someone is offended, and they're carrying an undisguisable grudge against another person who's present, and the atmosphere is sour. Everyone feels it, until not only those directly involved but everyone in that space can barely think or function, so thoroughly has the animosity poisoned the air — that was how it felt to Bailey and Steve.

"They're really pissed off," said Bailey, aware that this didn't even come close.

"Hatred," said Steve. "My god, they really hate us."

Neither had ever experienced anything like it, but the most concerning aspect wasn't its palpable manifestation but the source: the ancestors. When the spirits of our nearest kin turn in hatred and fury, there's no stronger possible signal of wrongness, and, lacking their good will, there seemed no means of continuation without offending them further. Steve and Bailey aborted the ritual and solemnly banished the room, ending with the traditional formula: "We thank you for your presence and give you license to depart. As you return now to your habitation, may there be peace between us."

Free at last to leave the circle, Steve went to the door and searched for any trace of a caller, but shouted back to Bailey there was none. They stepped out into the garden for a break, hoping the atmosphere in the lounge would, in the meantime, dissipate.

The messages from the ghost box had seemed to indicate they might be ignorant of something important, and at risk of harm. "But surely, they're not pissed off because I'm moving out," said Steve. "I mean, why would they care?"

"It felt like hatred, anger, offence," said Bailey, "as if they were disowning us, not our actions. It was personal."

"Yes," said Steve. "It felt like they were telling us we're not worthy of association with them, as if the past were rejecting the present. That makes a change, doesn't it?"

"Cancelled by our own ancestors," said Bailey. "Ouch."

Returning to the lounge, thankfully the atmosphere felt neutral again, but both understood that the results of magical workings are not synonymous with the immediate manifestations. Consequences had likely been set in train by the working, which, possibly, would unroll in unexpected ways. They'd asked for knowledge of things unseen, and things yet-to-be, and the ancestors had complied, but with every prophecy comes an obligation of making happen what has been foretold. Only by seeking the reasons for their ancestors' rage could the prophecy fully unfold. They might choose to do nothing, but that would be a novice error. The message they'd received had answered what had driven them to seek it. To assume nothing was required in return would be a gross rejection of the ancestors' favour.

They spent the night on the floor of the front bedroom, wrapped in sleeping bags. Tired by the work of shutting down the house, they slept more soundly than perhaps was justified by what had happened. Luckily, there was no rain that night. In the morning, they helped load the removal van. Steve was upbeat. Bailey was more withdrawn. Then it was all done, the house was empty, and it was time to hand in the keys, for Steve to leave his childhood home, and for them both to relegate to memory everything they'd done there.

"A new life and a new phase," Steve declared, as if it lay in his power to steer how the consequences of the ritual would unfold.

pylon

Bailey took a train to Leagrave. Outside the station, he asked a taxi driver to take him in the direction of Sundon. With hardly a word, the incurious driver complied. Bailey didn't mind; the lack of conversation afforded greater concentration on the route out into open countryside.

Before reaching Sundon, Bailey glimpsed through hedges the electricity substation, with its lines of pylons striding across the fields. The driver looked surprised when Bailey asked him to pull over, but once the fare was paid he drove away without comment.

Although the substation was hidden again behind trees, Bailey turned in its direction and discovered a footpath that seemed to promise the right trajectory. He descended some crumbling concrete steps onto a dry, mud track that formed a boundary between fields on either side. On his right and left, the hedges, trees, and shrubs had grown until they interlaced overhead. The afternoon was warm and breezy, but along this covered lane the air was still and cool. Flies whined, birds called, but apart from the rattling of leaves above him there were no other sounds, and no one in view. If the driver had asked why Bailey had chosen this remote and unremarkable place, he would've had to invent an answer because he didn't yet know. He was sure it wouldn't be for nothing.

There's never a zero outcome from magick, only unexpected ones. The closest to a null result would be to do nothing — but even that's an intention, from which outcomes are just as liable to manifest.

The track sloped gently downward, and, after a few minutes' walk, offered a ninety-degree turn that presented Bailey with a choice of turning right, down another leafy lane into what appeared a small village, or emerging from the trees onto a grassy footpath that led along the edge of a field. On the other side of that field was the substation. He paused, checking if his gut feeling was the same. A squirrel swirled in alarm, up and around a tree nearby, the only warm-blooded creature he'd seen so far. Stepping into the open field, he heard the drone of the substation, rising and sinking on the breeze. As he approached, it slowly gained in volume. Beneath the drone, there was a faint fizz and crackle, as if the electricity were hiding inside a musical disguise. Even though they sounded unalike, it reminded him of the ghost box: they shared in common a feeling of intelligence because, when you listen in a certain way, every sound is a voice. The hum of the substation was the electricity's marching song; the sound of power taking on a location and direction.

He reached the perimeter fence, a cage of tall and pointed metal stakes, with notices warning trespassers of hefty fines and instant death. Last week, from the distant train, in the gloom of the downpour, this place had looked sententious, but now, for the first time after deciding to act upon the feeling that he must come, he was doubtful. Magick, like sex, is a desire that visits sometimes at inconvenient moments, and is difficult to reignite if it's postponed or delayed. Although he couldn't, right then, sense it as strongly as he had, he knew he wouldn't be there if something hadn't called him. He would have to trust his feeling that it had.

The substation was just a substation: bigger than many, but nothing here presented any mystery, despite him having no idea how those geometrical arrangements of metal and cable worked, or what they did. On the train, he'd supposed there was something to discover: perhaps this was vital infrastructure on which the UK depended, or maybe it was on a target list in Russia or China, earmarked one day for a tactical nuke. But where it was or what it might perform didn't feel the point. What called to him must've depended upon the gloom and mizzle of that evening, because on this quiet and sunny afternoon, it had gone, and it seemed as if he must rediscover it.

On his left was more of the perimeter fence. On his right, a copse above which cables feeding from the substation dipped, and were lifted on its other side by a pylon that towered above the trees. Bailey headed towards the copse, following a track that suggested walkers occasionally passed through. He pushed deeper inside and found a space not too densely overgrown, with foliage between himself and the trail. He could sit here, unseen.

He took off his jacket and rolled it into a makeshift zafu that he tucked beneath himself, crossing his legs into meditation posture. He let himself settle, and then gently spread his awareness into the surroundings. The rustling of leaves masked the drone of the substation. The breeze was cool upon his face and hands, and the dry, dead twigs beneath him prickled through his jeans. From high above he became aware of a subtle whisper of wind through cables and a faint, electrical fizz from the pylon.

Her presence loomed over him. Pylons are female, and he knew he wasn't alone in sensing this: "nude giant girls" was their description in Spender's famous pylon poem. Of course, they were steel and sexless, but the shape of a pylon is undeniably evocative, as if broad-hipped, thick-thighed, with strength by necessity in the lower body.

He was hiding in a bush, thinking nonsense. But — no. He brought his mind back. What his mind found was what was there: breeze, undergrowth, drone, prickle, fizz. He had been called here, and he knew that if he put his awareness into this landscape then it would reciprocally enter into him. Attention is interpenetration, which can't be given without its recipient entering the mind just as deeply as the mind reaches out.

The giant pylon, with her many sisters, took the burden of the cable and carried the trapped lightning across the land. Bailey felt her strength and patience. She was waiting, and she could wait for a very long time. Below him, in the earth, he sensed faint vibrations, distant shocks, sensations that without the mental stillness he'd cultivated he never would've perceived. Behind his closed eyelids, alternating waves of colour washed: a shining, bluish purple, succeeded by verdant, brilliant green. He held his concentration at this level, where neither inner nor outer perception was more vivid. There were no thoughts about what he saw, because thoughts were things too, but if awareness of his body became attenuated then that was going too far, and so he'd re-ground himself in physical sensations, because what he found in this particular state of mind was what he wanted.

The tremors in the earth led him to a vision of a giant made of rock. Parts of the giant were free, but most of him was locked in deep, subterranean strata. For millennia, he'd strained against his prison. The ancestors had felt his struggle and had avoided this land. One day, he would break loose, but, until then, his despair tainted the ground. Bailey felt the giant's contortions and fury. As below, so above: the electricity trapped in the cables overhead also strove to be elsewhere and, as dangerous as the giant, it would seize any chance offered it to make a calamitous escape.

Bailey realised why the substation was here. Its planners were unconscious of the reason, or would have couched it in their own terminology, but the buried giant's frustration had called it: the law of like calling unto like. Less clear was why Bailey himself had been drawn, so he sank deeper into trance. His method was to focus on nothing, the non-place from where thought and perception originate, and into which they return. Everything appears from out of that nothingness. Bailey watched this in action, seeing how nothing else is happening, ever, other than nothingness ceaselessly contradicting itself, in an endless gesture of what might be described as love, compassion, repeated through every moment, when, maybe just as easily, it could have chosen not to.

His being was a contradiction of nothing. To take nothing in mind was to reveal himself as always falling away from it. Falling away, always and always, in everything he perceived or thought or did. He was far now into the real nature of things, but what he was seeking wasn't to be found there. This was theurgy, and although that was where all magick led ultimately, it wouldn't yield the answers he wanted. So, he grounded himself in sensations again, bringing awareness back to the qualities of that place. The light had changed as the afternoon wore on. He'd sat so quietly and still that a flurry of wings fanned his face and a bird dropped, unafraid, hopping about in bracken nearby. From behind, a couple of times, he'd heard stirrings that might be a squirrel or rabbit.

He focused again on the interpenetration of self and place, because magick was possible there. Ideally, he would have sat over several days, but all he had was a couple of hours. It didn't necessarily matter, because, in principle, a human being may enter any mental state at any moment. Sometimes, of course, certain conditions are needed, but mental change never precisely obeys causation. Success, at the type of magick he was working, would most often come from forsaking it entirely, because more powerful than striving to make a thing happen is simply giving up on preventing it.

Behind his eyelids, in the random shimmer of phosphenes, he sought out the central patch that glowed and fizzed with a hazy, purplish colour. The more he fed it attention, the more definite its outline became and the brighter it shone. The trick was to focus neither so weakly that this spot didn't appear, nor too rigidly that — when it slipped away, as it would at moments — its vanishment became more palpable than the possibility of its return. When the spot was there, he poured upon it all his attention and adoration, and it rewarded him by scintillating in a gleaming, metallic purple.

He was seeing what couldn't be seen. There was no object, no spot, apart from an interaction between his intention to concentrate and the physiology of his eyeball. It was not a perception nor a mental image; this was magick, designed for receiving visions.

Nearby, an old piece of wooden board lay flat in the bracken. He bent, and, flipping it over, caused a cascade of soil and dry leaves. Clinging to the other side, gelid and pulsating, was a giant grub, over a foot in length. Before he could flinch with disgust, the vision was gone.

Minutes later, on filament-thin legs, an insect picked a slow and fussy path through the leaf litter. Its body was iridescent green, and for a face it had two bulging compound eyes and a sharp proboscis, from which it exhaled a bright-blue vapour.

These were spirits of place, becoming visible because the landscape was entering him, the consequence of his attention entering into it. They were elemental spirits, their appearances a curious aggregate of the local biomass: aspects of caterpillars, worms, maggots, flies, and ants. Some might call them faery. Bailey wasn't sure. They seemed absorbed in their own business and, if they saw him at all, gave no indication.

It was hard to gauge the passing of time. No more visions came. The purple spot had vanished, and the visual field swarmed with monochrome specks, like an old analogue television tuned to an empty channel. This torpid state he knew only too well. He widened his focus to embrace the total width of his visual field, the whole length and depth of it. He looked upon it, yet felt tuned out from it, in a fuggy, buzzy kind of way. This was a state in which nothing would happen except for his consistent failure to stop wishing it would.

There was a guy Bailey had noticed around the streets where he lived. This guy wore tiny, pleated skirts and thigh-high socks. Often, this person was out with his girlfriend, and sometimes they wore matching outfits. Bailey wished he weren't thinking about him. Quite possibly he didn't identify as male. But the thoughts about this person kept returning, and about the girlfriend who went around with them. Maybe she didn't identify as he assumed either. Without knowing who identified as what, he couldn't think anything about them that wasn't his own assumption and might have caused them upset. How strange, that in putting on a skirt and socks to express who they were, someone rendered themselves less perceivable.

There was supposedly a waiter in London's Café Royal who asked his manager about the strange man in the pointy hat and cloak, embroidered with weird insignia. "That's the famous magician, Mr. Aleister Crowley, practising being invisible," he was told.

These nothing-happening states could stir the mind's undercurrents, where thoughts circled back upon themselves, and it was murky, crazy, and all of it: assumption. Every identity was a falling away from what a person really is. He thought of that enigmatic fragment from Heraclitus: "It is the nature of things to hide themselves." Maybe its meaning was lost in translation, or perhaps it, too, was describing how things become themselves by falling away from their true nature.

Certainly, Bailey would admit he hid, so that he could be what he wanted. He'd never pursued a career. He made a living from indexing scholarly books, and sometimes worked shifts in call centres providing mental health support to corporate employees. Money was always possible, but harder to secure was free time, and no one would pay him for what he wanted to pursue because consciousness cannot be bought or sold. Attention, on the other hand, is always vulnerable to being diverted and stolen. The struggle was always for control of where he put his attention and when. Wherever attention went, consciousness could follow.

Bailey's strategy had been to minimise his involvement in mainstream pursuits. He'd compromised on work, relationships, housing, but wasn't concerned that he'd never own a home. He put his effort instead into trying to be a decent person to live with. He'd lodged for five years with Steve, and for even more with his current landlord, who charged a modicum rent to share the house because Bailey was reliable, agreeable, and mostly unobjectionable. What he saved on rent enabled him to work less, and, in the time this granted him, he could direct his attention to wherever he wanted it to go.

Steve's approach differed. It was sometimes a source of friction between them, for whereas Bailey avoided the mainstream, Steve was unwary of diving in. "They're not exclusive," he told Bailey, "because you can just use the mainstream in the service of your magick," and Bailey couldn't deny how the house that Steve inherited, and which his full-time job maintained, was a case in point, and served them both well.

"It's not as if I'm living on the street," Bailey countered. "I go to work, and I pay my taxes."

"But you could provide more for yourself than that."

"I don't need to, and, besides, work's a con trick."

"I see it more as a game," said Steve. "Play it carefully and you'll be okay."

"Who sets the rules? If I was given the choice, I'd not play at all."

His thoughts had come untethered, and he'd drifted far away. Returning attention to bodily sensations, his legs, arse, and back were aching, and he badly needed to piss. Drifting away was always the main pitfall presented by the nothing-happening state. He was often led away by memories, apparently random, but with an emotional charge; and so too, snippets of remembered conversations, and imaginary arguments that never happened. But weirdest of all were dreams from years ago, some of which, originally, he'd forgotten on waking, yet here they were again, re-emerged and whole.

He opened his eyes and took a break. The sunlight, more oblique now, penetrated deeper through the foliage. He stood, stretched, then walked a short distance to urinate. He'd not seen or heard a soul all afternoon.

Returning to sit, he closed his eyes and found, again, the glowing spot. Perhaps because of the sunlight, which strobed gently against his eyelids through the fluttering leaves, the spot had changed colour to a greenish gold. Feeding it all his attention, it gleamed with the intensity of molten metal.

The torpid state of mind persisted, only now it didn't bother him. His thoughts still drifted, but with less commitment and energy than before. Quite possibly, he'd leave this place none the wiser as to why he'd been called, but, if he left as clueless as he'd come, then he and Steve would try to find the reason for the ancestors' anger by another route. It was enough to have heard the call and answered, to have met some spirits of place, and to have looked upon this gleaming, molten gold.

This was neither boredom nor numbness, because those are unpleasant, and this was not, although neither was it blissful. In a way that wasn't bad, and yet also wasn't necessarily good, nothing mattered. There was no attraction to any feeling or sensation, although these appeared as clearly as ever, but seemed to move on more quickly, with less fuss than usual. He wasn't holding onto the experience of things as tightly because, from where he saw them now, there was no need, and yet he felt a hazy listlessness. *If I'm not gripping onto anything*, he wondered, *then where is all my energy going?*

Something had happened to the spot: it had bloated into strange patterns glowing the same greenish gold, faded slightly, then morphing into a new pattern that shone brightly, and then the cycle repeated. He watched in detached fascination, the endless variety of patterns unfolding. They were sigils, formed of unknown characters from alien alphabets, combined with fragmentary sequences of geometric shapes — circles, angles, cylinders — and stylised glyphs of human faces, or peculiar animals, all jumbled together. It was how he imagined Aztec writing to be: hieroglyphics mixed with crenelated lines and figures. A historian of Central American civilisations, no doubt, would have angrily set him right, but the sense of a codified communication remained, at once ancient and culturally remote, as if something were signalling from a place neither within his mind nor outside.

Absorbed in the endlessly recombining sigils, he was completely uncertain now of how much time had passed. He had no wish nor expectation, no preference for things being one way nor another. With feeling, thought, and will suspended, his understanding unfolded to a different mode of being.

A breeze stirred the undergrowth, but was only a forerunner, a localised eddy, of a gust gathering in the further distance. It was coming. Already, it swirled the treetops and then, stronger, sighed overhead through the cables and the pylon's outstretched arms. It swooped down through the foliage to Bailey, as if seeking him. It stirred the leaf litter in a spiral around him.

Behind and above he felt the arrival of a vast and magnificent presence: the pylon. She'd waited until he was opened at last to her loving and luminous presence. Standing astride the trees, she reached down through the turbulent air and touched his heart. For one exquisite moment he vanished and was utterly gone.

Everything from me and everything to me, it seemed she was saying. *I am mother and lover both. I hold all in my embrace.*

A goddess, he realised. The pylon was her effigy; a stand-in. But then, swept up still in the overpowering bliss of her presence, he sensed the instigation of a different trajectory — as when an ocean liner changes course, and the captain's intention is clear, yet the execution of the manoeuvre takes a long, long time — so Bailey's heart shifted inexorably, excruciatingly, towards a sense of dread. She was about to reveal a terrible truth to him; he felt it, and even though it hadn't yet arrived, it was way too late now to avoid it.

Everything you have shall be taken away, she said. *All that you fear shall come to pass.* But even as the devastation of her prophecy swept through him, he understood this was preparation for a deeper, stranger truth. *Though it all passes away*, she seemed to say, *I shall hold you. The loss of everything is the form of my embrace.*

The final eddies of the breeze died away. He opened his eyes and the vision had ended. He heard again the drone of the substation — as if it had been interrupted and only just returned. The pylon was a pylon again. It hadn't really been about the place at all; it wouldn't matter if he never came back. Not in a long time had he felt something as real or intimate as this contact with the goddess. He didn't know her name, or who or what she was. But she seemed to know him, and that was all he needed.

pareidolia

Donna lay face down, snoring gently. Steve, beside her in the bed, wondered if she were dreaming, and wondered what kind of dreams she had. Although in endless variations, it seemed to him that everyone, perhaps, has a limited set of dreams.

One of his was the dream of putting on a play, usually with people from work, or with old university friends, or with people at school. The play was always Shakespeare, and though there hadn't been much time to rehearse (sometimes there was no rehearsal at all), everyone pulled together and the play was a brilliant success. He would wake feeling elated.

Another that buoyed him up (which he wouldn't, any time soon, be sharing with Donna) was the dream of meeting a new woman, unlike anyone he'd ever known, who was attracted equally to him, and who it felt he'd known for his entire life. He'd then wake suffused with sensations of newness and goodness so intense they rivalled the feeling of being in love in waking life.

But recently, perhaps every night, it was the dream of discovering long-forgotten rooms inside the old house. Even before he'd moved out, it had taken hold, from around the same time he and Donna first began talking seriously about buying a place together.

In the dream he was back there, alone — or, sometimes, with Bailey as his lodger — and it would be evening, or a dull, winter afternoon. Something would entice him into paying more than usual attention to ordinary things, such as getting up to turn on the light. But he would discover that the switch was not where it ordinarily was, and in looking for the switch he'd discover he was in another room entirely, long ago forgotten, which had just now reappeared.

More recently he encountered his parents living in these old but freshly rediscovered places. Mum appeared younger, looking the way he didn't remember her except from photographs taken when he was a baby. She would be knitting, or reading, or concentrating upon some household chore. She would look up and smile, and seem happy he'd found his way to wherever she was.

Dad he'd find working on or changing each room or space Steve discovered him in. Last night, in a room he hadn't stepped into since childhood, Steve found Dad building a library: empty bookshelves covered the walls from floor to ceiling. "Now you can move all your old books in," Dad smiled, and gestured, indicating to Steve he could take a portion of the library for himself. But, in the dream, Steve decided that rather than place his books in a separate area, he'd prefer to mix them in with the others Dad had built shelves for. It would be easier to find books in a single library than to search through different collections.

Strangely, no matter where they were, Steve found his parents in separate places, but in life they'd shared the same space for decades, right up until near the very end, when Mum was in and out of hospital. Before then, there hadn't been a moment when they'd ever been apart. In their solitary dream apartments, they seemed happy enough, but

the oddness of it haunted Steve. Death, it seemed, had altered them.

Dreams are thought of as things not really having happened. But they do happen, and really, in a way no different from thoughts and feelings — which don't always trans-
late into external world events but are not, for that reason,
regarded as if they never occurred. We assume in dreams
there's thinking going on, and seeing, and feeling, but really
there's none. Our eyes are shut, our mind is unconscious.
The senses, in dreams, reveal a non-physical world, and
Steve wondered if this were why dreams about the dead
are special. Although they are physically gone, the dream
senses can reveal them: seeing the unembodied requires
non-bodily eyes.

It will be strange, thought Steve, to be without a future.
Like weightlessness in outer space, except drifting in all
he'd ever thought, felt, and experienced. Maybe it would
be different from dreaming. When he was dead nothing
more could happen, so dreams would no longer be re-
sponses to events, but rather the absolute horizon of experience. This would explain why his parents now appeared
as dwelling in separate apartments. They must be dreaming,
because if this were Steve's dream and not theirs, he surely
would have dreamt of them together.

Donna had woken and regarded him, but he'd been too
absorbed in his thoughts to notice. "Hey," she said, "are you
okay?"

"Fine," he smiled. "I've been dreaming again. The old
house. Mum and Dad."

"You're missing them, and no wonder," she said.

He'd told her about the dreams, and how they felt, but
he hadn't mentioned the word that fully captured it: homesickness. They'd moved only a few weeks ago, and he knew

it would probably soon fade. Still, over the past few days, the pangs had grown stronger: a deeply felt urge to return to the old place. Of course, he couldn't; it was sold, and he had nothing to go back to. He didn't want Donna to think that he was regretful. Truly, he wasn't, and he was sure it would pass. So, until it passed, he would frame the feeling as just an adjustment to change, rather than admit a craving for what was left behind.

Homesickness hurt. It was a physical ache that, at its worst, induced a restlessness in body and mind from which he could not find focus or ease. The last time he'd felt like this had been at university, despite returning home frequently. But he'd never felt it since, because he'd lived nowhere other than in the old house.

He didn't want Donna to think the move had made him ill. It was such a pathetic malady. He found himself remembering and craving like an addict the smell of the cupboard under the stairs: leather, damp fabric, shoe polish, and darkness. Who uses shoe polish these days? Nevertheless, somewhere inside him its precise odour lingered. When his parents were alive, the understairs cupboard was filled with junk — things with no other place to go — like the sewing machine, Dad's huge, old suede suitcase, and the clothes horse. Steve missed the commotion of gestures demanded to hang up his coat in there, or take it out: the strain and struggle of having to reach through all the junk, and the chunky feel of the Bakelite switch he unthinkingly flicked on or off every day.

We use "pareidolia" to describe how the mind discovers specific forms in random physical appearances. In the old house, Steve saw faces in the garden wall, the Artex ceiling of the lounge, and electrical sockets in certain rooms. Most, he'd discovered as a child. Pareidolia can be transitory, but for Steve, over decades, the faces had become solid presences: like the one in the garden wall, a stern and protective hawk, who looked not unlike the Muppet character Sam Eagle, and sometimes seemed a little cross despite benign intentions.

The faces in the Artex were less defined, but he knew how to find them. Most appeared afraid or distressed, but even as a child he'd understood their feelings needn't define his. Sometimes, he'd seek them out to give them solace or commiseration, and he sensed that it brought them comfort. Their expressions never changed, but perhaps it was enough that someone saw them and cared.

He could never explain it to anyone, but he missed the faces. A house without such presences could be a home for the body, perhaps, but not quite for the soul. He hoped to discover faces in the new house, but suspected it might be a childhood power that he'd lost. It was sad to think of the old faces back there, betrayed by his abandonment, unnoticed by the new owners. He worried even for the face on the power socket in the back bedroom, which had the look of an aging boxer with a black eye, who'd always appeared as if he could survive any trauma. Steve hoped he was doing okay.

"I'm all right," Steve said. Donna looked at him searchingly. "Really," he said. "But, you know when you're a teenager, and everything about your parents is embarrassing: what they say and how they do things — it's all excruciating...."

"I'm not sure I ever had it quite the same, but I know what you mean."

"Yours had professional jobs, didn't they? Maybe it was a bit different. I don't know; perhaps you didn't feel as educated away from yours as I did."

"Maybe not as much," Donna agreed.

"Even so, we all go through it as teenagers, but later it settles down, and we realise our parents were just being normal adults."

"Because, presumably, we've become that too."

"Right," said Steve. "Well, I feel like I'm going through that all over again. Only, it's not just how they were that I'm having to come to terms with, but a certain way of being, a set of values."

"Isn't the whole point that we arrive at those independently of our parents?" asked Donna.

"I think I did," said Steve, "but now I'm wondering if I should've."

There was a thing his dad used to do, every year, which used to make Steve seethe. On the morning of Christmas Day, without fail, Dad would go to the pub, leaving Mum to make the dinner. But that wasn't the thing. Steve would wait, and then brace himself for the inevitable conversation at the dinner table when Dad came home.

"Guess who I saw down the pub," Dad would say to Mum.

"Who?" Mum would obligingly ask.

"Bill," Dad would say — or it might be "Jeff," or "Dave," or "Maureen."

"Oh," Mum would say, and there the conversation ended.

That was the thing, and as he grew older Steve couldn't contain his exasperation. "Is that it?" he'd protest. "You saw Bill. So, what about Bill? Did you say anything to him? Did he say anything to you?"

"We said hello," Dad would say.

"Where is the point in you telling us this?" teenaged Steve would rage.

"I don't know."

"Literally, the same every year," Steve explained to Donna. "I don't think he ever understood why it irritated me so much."

"But you understand now why he said it?" asked Donna.

"I think so."

"Well," smiled Donna, "you'd better tell me, because I don't get it, nor why it pissed you off so much."

"Suppose we went to the pub, me and you," said Steve, "and we bumped into one of your friends, but all we said was 'Hi,' and then we sat in silence at the same table and drank our drinks."

"That would be weird," said Donna. "A bit rude."

"Not where I grew up, you see. Everyone had similar lives, so you didn't have to make interesting conversation, because there's no point asking what someone's doing when you already know it's the same as you."

"Sounds dull."

"That's why it used to exasperate me."

"So, do you want me to be like everyone else?"

"No," laughed Steve.

"You don't want to go out drinking with my friends?"

"Not what I'm getting at," said Steve, but Donna looked unconvinced.

"It all seems a bit insular," she said. "Closed-minded. Narrow horizons."

"Yeah. And again, that's why it irritated me." He was thoughtful for a moment. "Where I've arrived at with it now," he said, "is that difference is a good thing, but I'm not sure that regarding ourselves as different is quite so good.

Mum and Dad never did, and that's what I miss. We've been educated into thinking that what makes us different is what's important about us."

"But without that no one would be allowed to stand out," Donna said.

"Well, I stood out at school because I was always quite clever," said Steve, "and I liked writing essays, so I decided I wanted to be a journalist when I left. One day, the teacher asked the class what everyone wanted to be, and a lot of the kids said they were going to be van drivers or working for one of the local firms, like their parents did. When I said 'Journalist,' the teacher said: 'What does everyone else think of Steve wanting to do that?' One of the boys at the back stuck up his hand: 'He's never going to get a job like that, is he Miss?' She let that stand and carried on with the lesson."

"That's horrible," said Donna. "She should have encouraged you, not undermined you. But you've just contradicted yourself because you were different: you were gifted."

"I was above average, maybe," said Steve. "It's only recently I've understood that calling a clever working-class kid 'gifted' is actually quite fucked-up, as if intelligence were rarer, proportionally, among the working class. Maybe she thought a dose of reality would do me good, but then she should've stated it herself, rather than leaving it to one of the class morons, who I never took seriously."

"Contradicting yourself again!" Donna laughed.

"Whatever," said Steve. "I was just being myself, but maybe she thought I was trying to be different, so the irony is that perhaps she was thinking along the same lines as I do now."

"You and Bailey lived pretty much on the same street, and went to the same school, so presumably he thinks the same."

"Bailey gets it," nodded Steve, "but he's always tried to stay out of life's way, whereas I never have."

"You sure?" smiled Donna.

"The clue's in our names, isn't it? Steven Chambers. Adrian Bailey. A chamber is a place hidden away indoors, and to get inside a bailey you have to blast down a castle wall."

"What's the story of his mysterious girlfriend?" said Donna. "Every time I've spoken with him, he's never mentioned her once. But you've met her, right?"

"Ex-girlfriend. He still sees her."

"If you're seeing each other, and neither of you are seeing anyone else, then you're still together," said Donna.

"They go back a long way," said Steve. "They met at uni and hovered around each other, but nothing much happened. Then they fell out of touch, but, after Bailey moved out from mine, by coincidence she was living in Brighton too, and they got together."

"Quite a coincidence," said Donna.

"Birds of a feather," said Steve. "He moved down there for a job. Apparently, she was already quite different from how he'd known her at university. She wasn't leaving the house much, even then. He told me the other week that it's now been over two years since she last went outside."

"Oh my god," said Donna.

"Yeah," said Steve. "I think he feels too guilty to leave her, and I suspect he might have made her a promise that he'll stick around."

"She doesn't leave the house at all?"

"Nope. That's how she was when I saw her."

❧

Donna couldn't imagine never leaving the house. No one could possibly want that, she reasoned, unless they wanted something else more strongly. She wondered if Bailey had fallen into a trap, fulfilling his girlfriend's underlying wish to be looked after and waited upon. Donna knew all about those traps, and how they were sprung, so quietly and surely that the person inside wouldn't notice. She knew about the manipulations the traps were made from, which ranged from subtle to violent. There had been times when she herself hadn't left the house for long periods, and she'd believed back then that she hadn't wanted to, but it wasn't true: she'd not been allowed out, because he hadn't trusted her — not Steve, of course, but her ex, whose name she still couldn't bring herself to say. There had been no warning signs when they met because he'd taken care to hide them. Only the stupid ones gave themselves away, and she no longer blamed herself for missing what he'd not allowed her to see. Rather, what she understood now were her own inclinations: what had attracted her to him was precisely the blankness, the emotional silence he'd concealed himself behind, but at the time it had looked to her like self-assurance, a mature composure and calm.

Donna's parents split when she was young. There had been tension and loud arguments before it came to light that Dad was seeing someone else. No one in the family had ever seemed able to hold Dad's attention. Donna and her sister struggled to remember a time he'd shown them genuine interest. It had taken Donna a long time to realise that the cool aloofness, which often attracted her to someone new, was, in fact, old and very familiar. Steve was not like that. After they first met, she'd had to make conscious efforts to reciprocate the interest in her he clearly showed. There was no mystery to him at all, which was why — she supposed — he was so keen on the occult and everything obscure and weird. Maybe he wasn't so obvious to everyone, but compared to her exes he was lit-up and open like a city at night. As if that weren't enough, he had a habit of always denying precisely whatever it was that he didn't want her to see.

She knew he was sick with grief at the loss of his parents' old home, and that he was doubting whether he'd made the right choice. She couldn't claim to understand it, and neither was she pleased, but, because he clearly didn't want to feel this way, or upset her by revealing it, she wasn't angry with him, nor too worried. While she knew better than he did what was going on in his mind, kindness and patience was all it would probably take to nudge him in the right direction.

Steve's phone played a burst of Mussorgsky's *Night on Bald Mountain*. "Speak of the devil," he said. "He must've sensed we were talking about him. Okay if I answer?"

"You don't need to ask permission."

"Hiya. What's up?" Steve said to Bailey.

Donna picked up a novel from the bedside table. It was about a group of friends and the impact upon their ideals and ambitions of Brexit, populism, culture wars, and ecological collapse. She was enjoying it so far. It felt good, sometimes, to slip into other people's problems and lose focus on her own.

"Yeah, all good here," Steve said to Bailey. "Yeah, she's fine, thanks. She's right here."

That was Steve's signal to Bailey to censor what they said, but she didn't mind. She was only half listening. The way that Steve and Bailey talked was like her sister, who had always been nerdy, possibly on the autistic spectrum. She liked *Dungeons and Dragons* and had nerdy friends she played it with. The way they discussed their games was how Steve and Bailey talked: treating what they imagined as if it were real. They were talking about what made their ancestors angry, and it seemed that Bailey was describing a visit to an electricity pylon, where he'd received a mystical vision of something bad.

It wasn't much different from reading a novel, she supposed. The real world is always imperfect, but as long as there's one foot kept planted inside it, then planting the other wherever you liked seemed to Donna no bad thing.

katabasis

Entrance to the underworld is gained by re-enacting its creation: this was the hypothesis that Bailey was testing. The underworld had taken its current form when Hades, its king, abducted the daughter of the earth goddess. Nothing would grow and the crops failed because the goddess of earth was so distraught.

Eventually, a deal was struck: her daughter would return for two thirds of the year, but, in the remainder, would rejoin Hades and reign as the queen of hell. This laid a pattern not only for the yearly seasons but also for interactions between the living and the dead.

Therefore, Bailey figured, there must be two ways in. One was the route the daughter took, snatched out of the world against her will: an involuntary route of abduction, rape, and trauma. This is the forced, irresistible path to hell that opens up whenever something terrible happens. Confronted with a choice between remaining in hell forever, or for one third of the time, the latter seems a reasonable deal.

The second way, less risky but no less dark, was the route the mother took: of loss, depression, and despair. When something precious is lost, the path into hell is followed to retrieve whatever can be salvaged.

Bailey wondered if the difference were only a matter of circumstances and personal disposition. The way of the daughter seemed more passive: better not to choose this one, perhaps, because to take it intentionally would mean having to put himself knowingly into harm's way. People living with PTSD, survivors of satanic abuse, or alien abduction — Bailey imagined those folk knew this route only too well, despite not having chosen it. Probably, they wouldn't wish it upon anyone.

So, he would follow the path of slower descent: the melancholy way of loss into the underworld to find the goddess who had called him. To her whom it would disrespect to name, because to name is to control, and the queen of hell is biddable by no one.

It was mid-morning, and his landlord was out at work. Bailey, in his room, made a banishing ritual, lit a long stick of incense, and then sat upon a cushion and closed his eyes. He sank, and in imagination sank deeper and deeper still. Proprioception, the body's sense of its position in space, is amenable to imagination; so, Bailey induced through imagination a sensation of his body falling into empty space, further and further down. He fed it with attention until it felt real, and his heart and pulse raced with the vertiginous sensation of falling uncontrollably, down and down, into endless depth.

He maintained this until his body relaxed and the effort of concentration dropped away, but his focus remained. In the centre of his chest it felt as if an aperture had opened. A feeling of excited love flowed out from his heart, at the same time seeming to flow inwards.

A spirit appeared on the right of his field of vision, a downward-pointed triangle glowing brightly magenta and yellow in concentric bands that radiated from its centre. It told Bailey it would guide him, and it explained the correct way down: Bailey must perceive the spirit in a way that made its radiance vanish.

What a mental image presents is one thing, but the image itself is another. Bailey adjusted his focus away from its contents and onto its form. Passing beyond colour, beyond shape, the triangle's radiance faded and its voice fell silent. As he passed beyond bodily sensations, the aperture in his chest glowed a vivid, pale blue. He was close to finding a way below. He was not there yet, but sensed how, in the underworld, the pale-blue fire in his heart would consume whatever it touched, and the ashes remaining would be dense and fertile.

He realised something had happened, but it was so far beyond form he couldn't say what it was or bring the meaning of it back. His disappointment over this had a form, and he felt that well enough, but he understood he might not perceive or remember everything that happened to him in the world of the dead.

As if in response, a vision arose. He'd descended into a small cavern with neither exit nor entrance, and, in the cavern's centre, exuding from his body a weak light, a child sat meditating. His name was Astyanax; his head was bald and grotesquely swollen, while his face was empty of all expression because of his deep trance. The cavern was projected from his head— sometimes what's self-evident in a vision feels impossible to describe. Astyanax was like a Möbius strip: the space around him issued from his mind, and then circled back into itself with no boundary. What seemed like a place wasn't.

Bailey realised that he was within the mind of another, which meant that he had not descended into the world of the dead. When he could sense what he did not need to be alive to sense, then he would know that he was there. He saw the technique he must use: he must make a way down only he could wriggle into, so specifically fitted to himself that no one else would find it. More so, this had to be without an intention ever to escape or return. No one alive would willingly accept such a condition, and this would cut him loose from the mind of Astyanax.

The method of bringing all this together was simple: he would descend to the dead by means of a secret. He suspected everyone had one: something never divulged, yet fundamental to a person's sense of identity. This offered a way down fitted only to him, and, while the secret remained undivulged, it separated him from every living person. By this means he had, in effect, renounced the world above.

He set the secret before him: what no one knew, and yet it defined him. It wasn't difficult to put into words. Letting it fill him, he slipped past the mind of Astyanax and sank down deeper.

Confused, he woke again from what he couldn't remember, and realised that once more he'd entered briefly into the world of the dead. Only a dim feeling remained of a long conversation — with someone unknown — about something forgotten. Nevertheless, it had happened. There had been a recognition or an acceptance, but whether in himself or in the unknown person he'd spoken with, it was unclear. But it could never have happened at all if he weren't now in the space beyond cognition, where the heart burns as a pale, blue fire.

In an iron cage high on the wall, an antique railway clock ticked slow and loud. Below the clock, a woman in Edwardian dress — a long purple skirt and matching hat, a white blouse and short, black coat — came to meet him as

the vision took hold. Her features flickered between appearances.

I can help you see more in the world of the dead, she told Bailey.

The tick of the clock slowed, which felt wrong, but the
presence of the woman comforted him. Immediately, she
noticed this.

Do not depend upon me, she warned. *It will play into the
sense of wrongness you feel.*

She was the container — it seemed she was trying to explain — and the container does not define the contained,
but it can be affected by its contents. *You are contained*, she
told him, *but what you misunderstand affects me also.*

The relationship was asymmetrical. She could help, but
he had to know himself for her to help him. He sensed she
knew his secret; if not, he wouldn't have made it this far.
There was something else he must recognise, something
affecting the way he perceived her. Help me understand
this, he implored. But, as when somebody says something
cruel or obscene or utterly unconscionable, and then a
shocked silence descends upon the company — awkward
and heavy, so that, in the moment, the impulse might be to
ignore that the words were actually spoken — likewise Bailey felt the wrongness expand and swell until it was too
palpable to discount or deny. The only option left was to
meet it with some kind of a response.

The woman stood silently while the clanking tick from
the clock above their heads resounded ever more slowly.
Bailey realised she was waiting patiently and uninsistently,
but what felt wrong was her detachment from any inclina-
tion to intervene. Yet, she remained there, looking on, even
as she refused him any guidance, encouragement, or care.
Complaint and hurt welled up within him, but her quiet

patience stalled and withered his recrimination, and he understood this was not intransigence. Something strange and difficult confronted him; maybe something unbearable.

Her silent waiting, he understood, was like a vigil at the sickbed of someone dying. Incredulously, he thought: She is keeping watch, and I am dying. She is waiting for me to die.

It was cruel abandonment, and incomprehensible, that she could consider it appropriate, but, after a moment, it struck him how, in such circumstances, it was equally wrong to presume to help, to try to fix or enervate the dying. He was mortal, she was not; this was indeed a death-watch, and she was keeping vigil. The feeling of wrongness collapsed, because her patient waiting was actually a kindness. What had made it feel bad was his own unmet desire. To navigate these realms as a mortal being, he would have to let go of his longings and the need for acceptance. Living beings connect to each other through their desires but, as the woman had tried to explain, with the dead or spiritual beings the relationship is asymmetrical. Human need prevents us from meeting them fully. This was the reason he and she were standing in silence, waiting beneath a railway clock; she, with infinite patience and kindness, until Bailey discovered the proper means to die.

But a vision doesn't end because it's not understood. Although nothing further happened between Bailey and the woman, except that she waited, and her waiting was a kindness, within the limits of the understanding he'd so far gained, he was shown the workings of the place in which he found himself.

It wasn't, as he'd surmised too readily from the clock, a station concourse. He saw concrete walls around him, concrete floors, vents, and metal piping, and consoles for machines that operated subterranean pumps. He knew it well from previous dreams he'd had, and realised the electricity substation at Sundon had been another instance of it in waking life. Into this underground industrial space, animals were brought, groups of animals, for the purpose of meeting other groups. It occurred regularly, and felt too functional for a ritual, yet lacked the practical purpose of science. Nature encountered other natures here: a group of one species met another, and both would depart changed and wiser. The pipes and pumping facilitated the underlying principle: through encountering what it isn't, something takes inside itself the nature of the other. It seemed to Bailey he was being shown how the purpose of every machine, from the hand axe to artificial intelligence, amounted to the movement of attention from place to place. Every machine was an attention pump, enabling mental focus to shift and meet something other than itself. In this sense, all machines serve the purpose of encouraging animals to meet.

Enough. He was losing coherence. He opened his eyes and crashed out of the vision into his room. Hazy sunshine gleamed through the window. He heard again the swishing rhythm of cars along the road. It was nearly lunchtime. He inhaled, and let his mind re-adjust to the sensory world. There had been so much in the vision, it had almost felt too much.

Other worlds and states of being are traversed in magick, but it's always the everyday world to which we return. Whatever is gained is brought back here, and here it has to be lived with. It's a sure path to destruction when this is forgotten, because attempting to escape into those realms is like waving goodbye to living a human life.

He locked up the house and walked through terraced streets down into the city centre. He bought a burrito from a stall, plus a vegan, wheat-free option for Kristyn. This is the real world, he thought, looking at the shops, people, cars, roads. This is normal life. He knew reality is a quality, present in certain experiences, but not in others. He reflected on how, currently, he was trying to appreciate the reality of things, but he couldn't keep that up all of the time. If reality were truly as real as it's supposed, why is awareness of it not always there? Often by "real" what's actually meant is "how things ought to be."

Some would say his relationship with Kristyn wasn't "real." Steve, he sensed, thought that, and Bailey could imagine how Steve had described it to Donna. But no relationship, really, makes sense to anyone other than those inside it, and often not even to them. Donna's practicality, her frank materialism, was what Bailey imagined had attracted Steve — yet these were qualities he'd heard Steve declaim as repellent when he'd encountered them in others. So, Bailey concluded, Steve and Donna's relationship made no sense — but so what? That didn't mean it wasn't there, nor even that it wasn't working.

He descended the steps to Kristyn's basement flat, calling out as he let himself in with his key. Inside was pleasantly cool, but there wasn't much light, and — like most of the city's aging basement flats — it smelt faintly of drains. By now, he was well-used to navigating the piles of junk Kristyn kept in the hallway, and every other room. The bulk of it was old magazines, catalogues, mailshots; the rest was kitsch, most of which she bought online: plastic Japanese dolls; fairy lights; dreamcatchers, and other faux-indigenous artefacts. They were all things that might raise a smile or steal attention for a moment, but that no one would seriously contemplate buying, except Kristyn always did. It wasn't quite pathological hoarding — there was a clear path from the door, which turned left into the lounge, and continued on and into her other rooms — but he worried that maybe it wasn't far off. Sometimes, she would make a big scene about throwing some stuff away, but this mostly meant reorganisation. The overall volume never diminished.

Before he'd made it as far as the lounge, he could tell she hadn't washed. This he found hard, because as his disgust rose, so did his anger. If she'd been expecting another visitor, she'd have made the effort, and on those rare occasions, months ago, when occasionally she'd left the flat, she'd taken a shower. But for him, the person supposedly she was closest to, she seemed to want to make herself disgusting. There had been no physical intimacy for over two years. It was unthinkable now. Making herself stink was as blatant a rejection of that possibility as a punch to his face, and also an assault on whatever closeness endured. It wasn't as if he hadn't spelled out how it made him feel, or that it wasn't easily fixed if she so chose. Even though he'd plead with her sometimes to just go and take a shower, she'd fob him off with promises and excuses.

She was on the sofa, under a blanket, sipping herbal tea and watching a quiz show. "What are you doing here?" she said.

"We arranged to have lunch."

"Okay then."

"I've bought you a vegan burrito."

"But I'm wheat-free."

"I know," he said. "It's wheat-free as well."

She sniffed at the food and unwrapped it. There were dirty plates on the floor, and a bowl with the remains of that morning's cereal. It was mid-afternoon and clearly she hadn't had lunch, but she seemed to want to pretend she wasn't expecting him.

"You haven't had a wash, again."

"I was just going to have a shower, but then you came in."

"It's been a few days, Kristyn. I can tell."

The stink developed over time. First, it was like prawns when they start to turn. After, it sank into a darker, earthier reek that lingered on surfaces and objects she touched. (This was the stage she was at currently.) Out from there, it turned insane. He'd smelt something similar in the woods last summer, and on investigation discovered the rotted carcass of a deer.

"I'm guessing no one else has been around," he said.

She shook her head, eyes fixed on the television. Steeling himself against the stink, he settled next to her on the sofa, laying an arm about her shoulders. She shrugged with irritation, but snuggled against him and relaxed. They ate together, occasionally calling out answers to the quiz.

He hated to think of her alone in the flat, although at every opportunity she would signal that this was what she preferred. Nearly all her friends had given up. She was the wreckage of what she'd been, and he was the dreamer of a nightmare who flees around the corner from the monster only to find it waiting there for him: he felt that it was he who'd ruined her.

Her previous relationship had been abusive, and, prior to that, there had been a sexual assault by a co-worker. When they'd first got together, he'd sensed her caution, but it had touched him how, despite all she'd suffered, she had love in her enough to risk again intimacy with a man. Her trust deserved all the tenderness he could offer in return. Months passed, before she began to feel safe with him and could relax. It was more than worth the wait to watch her come alive. Her friends approved of him, but, really, all he'd done was to provide some affection and tried not to act like a prick.

Every relationship in its early days wears a golden halo which fades with time, but this needn't diminish its contentments; yet it seemed this one's very stability bred the conditions for its turning awry. The signs grew slowly: at first, Kristyn's reluctance to stay over at Bailey's place. She pleaded tiredness, and it was no big deal for Bailey to meet at hers instead. But soon, hers was the only place she'd tolerate, and Bailey found himself handing back — at her request — the overnight bag that she kept at his, her tacit signal she'd decided never to return.

Having found in Bailey someone she could rely upon, Kristyn seemed to retreat from the outer world into their relationship. He'd noticed early on that asking her to do something, or just expecting that she might, would elicit anger and defiance. At first, he'd found this endearing, a manifestation of a fiery independence. And perhaps, as she had accused, there had been latent sexism in how he'd expressed himself, so he took care with language when making requests.

She'd been between jobs when they started out, and slowly it grew clear that employers' demands provoked the same reaction as his; paid work, for Kristyn, had become an intolerable imposition.

She didn't have stand-up arguments with bosses. Instead, she took a bitter, silent path of non-compliance, resentment, and descent into recriminatory depression and psychosomatic illness. Gingerly, Bailey dropped suggestions he hoped she might pick up for self-employed or freelance ventures, which would minimise interactions with a boss. His suggestions worked only to the degree that some of them lit her imagination. She would resolve to follow them up, but that was as far as it went.

She allowed Bailey to be her buffer. He was working, almost full-time, and could supplement her sickness benefits with gifts and treats. But this was colluding — not helping — and he knew it. They might've lived together, but stretching his mediocre salary to cover them both seemed a miserable prospect; he would've had to commit to his employment and manoeuvre for a promotion, but he didn't want that. It would've meant less time for what interested him.

Looking back, Bailey saw this as the moment he should've left. It would've hurt, but it would've been more honest, because he'd recognised she was dependent upon him, yet he was ducking that responsibility. Nothing was spoken about it, things rolled on. Kristyn retreated from him and the world, and Bailey enabled her. After a bad bout of flu from which she insisted she'd never recovered, Kristyn announced she no longer had health or energy enough to leave the flat. Bailey took on her weekly shopping, and all her errands outside home, and so the pattern was locked in.

Nestled next to him on the sofa, without turning from the television, she said: "I had a weird dream last night, about a room in an office block, somewhere across town, where, every year, something amazing happens. A miracle. Every year, we used to go together to watch it, me and you."

"Sounds nice," said Bailey, careful to avoid giving any impression of having an opinion about the dream's meaning, which he knew would enrage her. "What kind of a miracle?"

"Something to do with animals being taken in and out," she frowned. "It was a weird part of town, near the railway. Lots of overhead wires and things."

"We went together?"

"We used to," she said. "We couldn't anymore because, in the dream, I was like I am now. But you insisted I had to go with you."

"Doesn't sound like me."

"You disguise how you're always making me do things," she said. "Actually, you're quite manipulative, but in the dream you just told me straight."

"So, what did you do?"

"There wasn't anything I could do, was there? You said you'd go alone, and that you weren't coming back. Then I woke up."

"Well, that really doesn't sound like me."

"Even in the dream," she said, "I knew you would come back. You can't ever leave, because you love me."

She'd dreamt the dream last night, yet it seemed filled with echoes from the future, of the vision he'd obtained only that morning, as if she'd intuited something were leading him away — but it would fail, because he was bound to her. Hearing her say it aloud, his heart sank. It was not love that held him; it was weakness and guilt.

The quiz show went on, and he called out the answers. Sometimes the world comes apart, but thinking and doing continue, perhaps because the world is never truly held together. The relationship had become so thinned it barely existed, yet he thought of her all the time, and the alternative seemed no better, because how would she cope? She felt warm and fragile beside him. He hugged her tighter. "I promised I wouldn't go away," he said, "and I'll stick to that."

nostalgia

Database administration is an occupation that generates anecdotes neither exciting nor hilarious. Steve rarely mentioned to Donna things that happened at work; her job, as a classroom assistant, provided far more material for their daily conversations.

Steve said almost nothing about what he did for the bulk of his day, nor about his esoteric interests outside of work. His parents had barely understood what he did for his living, but they were always pleased and proud that he had a decent and reliable income.

He remembered the day of his school exam results, after his dad came home to the news of Steve's success.

"Well done, boy," he'd beamed. "Now you won't have to work with these," he'd said, holding out his hands, "you'll work with this instead," and he'd pointed at his head.

Steve's parents always wanted a different life for him than theirs. It had taken a while, but now he was there. Donna was watching television downstairs, and he'd come up for something but now he couldn't remember what. So, he'd laid down for a rest, and then he'd started thinking, and soon it'd grown dark. He told himself that he'd go back down in a moment.

It must've been different, he mused, back in ancient days, or even a couple of hundred years ago. You'd have lived with the people closest to you, and you couldn't have not known all about them; you wouldn't have done for a living things that they couldn't understand, and parents wouldn't have wished difference upon their children. The further back in time, the more likely you'd be working with your family on the land. It must've been a trauma when people were forced out of the fields and into the factories. When did it start to feel normal that family members spent their days in separate places? Maybe, he thought, the harm it did is impossible now to recognise. Needing to work to raise a family is taken for granted, but from a human perspective makes no sense, and if it's not a human perspective we're looking from, then what are we doing?

Things were not great at work. His team was being outsourced again — for the fourth time. He'd worked in the same building for years, at the same job, only, supposedly, for three different companies, people he'd never met or seen. Mostly, the work consisted of patching up old systems that should've been replaced, propping them up with kludges and workarounds while, to the client, making the system appear the same even as it worsened. It was unlikely, but during an outsourcing there was a risk the new owner might call time on ripping off clients. More usually, however, it was the client who complained first. In either case, jobs on his team would probably be cut at some point. It seemed inevitable, one way or another.

Steve's career in computing had arisen not from a passion for tech, but because he found it easy; he'd done it because he could and, until recently, the pay had been decent. The new owners might decide they didn't need Steve's team at all, not since folks in India were offering the same work for cheaper. Steve wasn't convinced their bodges and hacks were up to the UK's standard — he'd seen code bought from a company in Mumbai: it worked, but in the same way as kicking down a fence solves the problem of climbing over it. The code looked to Steve as if it'd been written by someone young, sitting up too late at night on hyper-caffeinated drinks. A good coder is focused always on the question of what is the best way to achieve the task in hand. Steve held this constantly in mind, but, if he were honest, it wasn't a question that interested him much.

Maybe, he thought, everyone's approach to life can be summed up as a question they're trying to answer. In that case, the question that interested him most of all was: What is this? What is it really?

Coding was like a magical incantation for making something appear, so it was probably not coincidental, the sheer number of people Steve met on the occult scene who worked in tech. What coding and magick shared wasn't only the thrill of manipulating words and symbols to alter reality but, deeper, a common understanding that meaning is part of the fabric of reality; words and symbols aren't representations only, but real in themselves. Both during a magical ritual and inside a computer, words are actions, symbols are events.

It fascinated him how a computer could never be wrong. Of course, it could break, and, yes, its program might be faulty, but it would always run that program flawlessly: it was built in a way that meant it could not do otherwise. As an angel performs the will of God, he thought, without free will, but from something greater: the inability to fall short ever of what it must fulfil. Computers are material bits of kit, for sure, but perhaps we have made them in the image of angels. We have machines that work like spirits, yet what do we use them for? The reason the dead hate us, he considered, is that we're not fully alive, and so, in retaliation, they refuse to die.

What troubled him about the ritual with Bailey, despite (as he'd foreseen) no explicit indications, was the implied presence of his parents. In retrospect, hedging this had been stupid; they were ancestors, so of course they'd been likely come, but how had their lifelong support of him flipped into palpable antagonism? He felt it in ways he couldn't deny: homesickness, nostalgia, the recrudescence of grief he'd supposed resolved long ago. It amounted to this growing sense that he couldn't push through and simply enjoy living with Donna.

It was nothing she'd done but, if he mentioned it, he knew she'd consider herself a target of blame. Perhaps blamelessness was part of it: his parents were long-dead when he and Donna met, so she would never know how much his mum and dad would've loved her — especially his mum, who never disguised her longing for grandkids. "Oh, I can see her pushing a pram," his mum would've said if she'd met Donna who, to be frank, was quite maternal-looking and would've had kids years ago (Steve surmised) if her exes hadn't been such jerks.

His parents would've loved her, and he knew precisely how, and even though they never met Donna, their relationship with her existed in Steve's mind, exactly as it would've if they had; and, because relationships don't exist other than in the mind, it was as real as any relationship, despite its never having been lived. This, he'd come to know, was the nature of the dead: they'd ceased to live but hadn't vanished; they were still active in the world which belongs to them as much as to us.

Donna hadn't met them, so they weren't her dead. Donna wasn't there when Mum fell ill. She and Dad kept it quiet at first, not wanting to distract Steve from his uni studies. But when surgery fell due, this changed, and Steve helped Dad at home as Mum recovered, and then through the ensuing months of chemo, when sometimes Mum was rough. Donna hadn't lived through the ruthless optimism when, despite habitual caution, the consultant's prognosis wasn't looking too bad. But the cancer didn't listen and, after it returned, what hadn't been thinkable before they had to start to think. Donna wasn't there when accepting reality felt like betraying Mum, who faced it the best she could, never complaining of pain, but only when others went out of their way to help. What Mum couldn't disguise was her distress at the impact on Dad, who knew precisely what feelings Mum was hiding, and almost equally suffered inside himself.

When Mum's time came, friends and family all said they were coping remarkably well, which made it sound as if they were doing something, but the only thing happening was the cancer, and they were following in its wake. They arranged for her to be at home where, gradually, she became less and less, saying the same things over: that she loved them and they mustn't worry. Her words were coming from further and further away, demanding from her great concentration, as if she were striving to remember even what words were for. In her final conversations she seemed to be distracting herself from something that commanded an ever greater hold on her attention. Sometimes, a look of wonderment would cross her face; she'd seem surprised and would halt before rediscovering the words. "What was that just then, Mum? What did you see?" Steve asked. She looked blankly, seeming not to understand what he meant, but it gave Steve comfort, because even though she was receding it seemed there was something she was moving towards. He wished Dad felt it too, but Dad was run dry and ashen with horror and loss.

Donna hadn't seen any of this. She'd told Steve her view was very much there's nothing after death. Steve worried for her, that this belief would hobble and blind her, and when her own parents' time came it might, like his Dad, leave her vulnerable to despair. But Steve knew her well enough to understand that if Donna lacked anything it wasn't empathy. If she'd been at Mum's bedside she would've seen what he saw, and it would've changed her from how he knew her now.

The last couple of days, Mum was silent. She fell into what looked like sleep, assisted by the medication, except her breathing wasn't right: deep, snoring breaths that sounded mechanical, as if she'd gone away and left her body on automatic. Like a ghastly minimalist music, the tape-loop of her breathing over countless repetitions faltered and degraded, while Steve and his dad hung on, listening with dreadful fascination, until at last it reached its stop.

Death, having entered the house, over the months that followed never seemed to leave. After the funeral, Dad remained an imitation of himself, reluctant to see anyone, and reliant on Steve to cook, clean, and care. The first signs of his illness were misdiagnosed as low mood. Pancreatic cancer treated with antidepressants. Of course, Dad was depressed, but his cancer must've been advancing even before Mum died — although, irrationally, Steve was certain if Mum hadn't fallen ill then neither would've Dad. By the time Dad was diagnosed the benefits of treatment were negligible.

Mum had never complained of pain, and she'd certainly wanted to live, but Dad's lack of complaint was absolute. He withdrew into utter capitulation, and he waited to die with a matter-of-fact earnestness that it should be soon.

The change in Dad was what Steve would've wanted Donna most of all to have lived through with him. Life, for Dad, without Mum was impossible. He jumped on board his illness and rode to its destination like someone grateful of a timely bus.

Steve had no doubt his parents loved each other, and being in love, perhaps, is the most faultless state of being. But, if life is unliveable without the beloved, might turning away from everything be a failure of love? Steve didn't blame his dad for not caring enough to hold onto his life. In fact, he was thankful that Dad, as the end approached, was neither despairing nor afraid. Yet Dad left Steve with a question: if we love someone more than anything, might this be a betrayal of the world? When Dad gave up on his life, it was out of love for Mum, but maybe also from hatred at everything else. Steve knew Mum would've wanted Dad to live, as Steve had too, but, of course, it was neither his nor Mum's choice to make. Decisions are taken and, across time, what's left becomes questions for others to answer.

Donna believed the world was harsh, and so we owe it nothing, except we owe it to ourselves to be happy: that was what she'd said when he'd talked about what Dad's dying had been like. If she'd known Dad and lived with him through that time, then she'd have lived through the questions he'd bequeathed, and probably she would've arrived at different answers.

Steve wondered if the ideal of loving a person above all else was what had made Donna vulnerable to abusive men. The question her father's absence had left behind was whether she deserved attention, and perhaps unappreciative men were her attempt at a response. If she'd met Steve's dad, she would've known a man whose love was centred upon one woman, such that when she died there was nothing left. Donna might have seen that wherever her love shone, if it elicited no reaction then that wasn't a denial of its light. It proved only the dullness of what she'd directed it upon.

Steve lay in the dark, still. He ought to go downstairs and sit with Donna, but instead he rolled onto his other side. He may as well have called it a day, and slipped into bed, but he stayed where he was. A heavy weight lay upon him — only thoughts, yet of late they'd gained a power to pin him down as they spiralled about him.

He didn't pretend he saw clearly; the meanings of his dreams and ruminations were filtered through the lens of his past. The theme of his life, he supposed, was never leaving home, for he never really had, and he never had needed to. Because his parents had left him by dying, he'd never left them. He'd gone on living in their house with his oldest childhood friend until, perhaps, his love and attention — just like Dad's — had focused all in one direction. Now, he was reliant on Donna for change, but she couldn't make these feelings go away; she hadn't lived through what was needed to understand them and, even so, what he'd seen in her that could help him was hers alone. He couldn't take it from her, and she couldn't give it away. The best he could do was to change how he felt, but the feelings wouldn't change because, deep down, he still lived in his parents' house. In his dreams, when he returned there and discovered new rooms, or old ones he'd forgotten, it was a demonstration that he hadn't left. The dreams showed he must keep going back, because there was more to discover.

In a way, the dream couldn't be clearer, particularly the part that made no sense: his parents leading different lives in separate rooms. Dad would never have settled for an eternity of adjacency to Mum, but that was Dad when alive and perhaps Dad dead had different inclinations. If anything changes a person, reasoned Steve, probably it's death. When something is fake it tries to escape notice, avoids scrutiny, yet dreams are strange, so shockingly dissonant: it's as if they wanted to attract attention, perhaps towards something that's not untrue.

No, it was more than evident he hadn't left because Mum was here, knitting by the light of the table lamp. The clock by the lamp read three-thirty. It was a Saturday afternoon in November. Mum said: "You have avoided orthodoxy, so we have nothing to eat," which was like nothing she'd ever spoken, but he'd have to get used to his parents speaking and acting in weird ways, now that they were dead. He supposed she meant that he hadn't taken an ordinary course through life, yet why had she rebuked him for starving her? If he'd stuck to the mainstream they wouldn't be having this conversation.

"What's it like, Mum?" he asked. "Where are you? Are you happy?"

She made a strangulated noise and stared with bulging eyes. It was horrible — as if she were having a seizure — and he was frightened his question had hurt her. Her face and the weird noise became a repeating sequence of actions, as when a character in a game is mistaken for one that's significant and every attempted interaction provokes a meaningless response.

His questions, he realised, demanded an awareness of her current experience, but, being dead, she had none, and so the result was these grotesque noises and tics. He couldn't bear this creepy simulacrum, like a hollow shell with no interior. Mum was now the remnants of what she'd been, defined only by what she'd done, because — life having gone — there was no more doing.

He took her hand, focusing on its warmth, and her face —younger by a couple of decades than when she'd died — and the scent of her, and the felt sense of her physical presence. At once, the weird behaviours stopped. She saw him, smiled, and had returned, but, he realised, this was all she could be. She could be back, but, being dead, never again could she be alive with a present and a future.

Steve heard Dad calling from another room.

"What does he want?" sighed Mum and resumed her knitting.

"I'll see you again," said Steve, and no sooner had he turned to search for Dad than they were seated in armchairs opposite one another, within the library lined with books.

"I was always trying to take care of you," said Dad.

Steve didn't want a repeat of what happened with Mum, so he took time to phrase his question, but then found he didn't have one. What Dad had said was the answer to anything Steve could've asked.

"I know, Dad."

Like Mum, Dad's appearance dated from an earlier stage of life when he had plenty of hair and was ruddy with energy and health. There he sat, exactly as he'd been, nothing like his older self that had given up on life. If the dead have no future but only the power of return, then — thought

Steve — maybe that's no small thing, because they can come back from any moment in their lives.

"Why did Mum say she had nothing to eat?"

"Well," said Dad, "I, too, have not been all I could have."

The sayings of the dead were bizarre. They were doing something strange with language and time. Perhaps not having a future bound them to the past, or might it unbind them from any sequence of events? The words weren't what Dad would have said. At the time he'd died, he'd had no urge to go on, but now he was no longer speaking from inside his life. Maybe, thought Steve, when experience ends we speak from outside it.

The words sounded curiously like accusations he'd once harboured against Dad, in which case the answer Dad had given was Steve's own question. Hearing it from Dad's mouth, Steve realised what he'd once levelled at Dad applied mostly to himself. Steve had not been all he could have been. He hadn't moved on because his life was bound up too much with his parents. If only — in Mum's words — he'd embraced orthodoxy, maybe they could die properly. In their topsy turvy language he supposed that "eating" meant diminishment and fading away.

The language of dreams and the dead are the same. Nothing new or alive is spoken in either; nothing open to a future, because dreams are made from mixed-up fragments of what has happened and, likewise, the dead speak through appearances of what they were. Yet words, in dreams, resonate with sententious finality, as if nothing further could be added, which only makes it seem we cannot grasp them — when we do, we realise their meaning lands precisely on target. Dreams and the dead are so finished and done, so retrospective, that they lie outside of existence, outside of time.

Words spoken in dreams are more than adequate, so he sat in silence opposite Dad, relishing his presence. If the appearance was Dad's, and if it looked, felt, smelt, and behaved like him, then where was the difference from the actual man? The dead have the power of return, but the power of the living — thought Steve — is to direct attention; really, he thought, it's all that we can do. He understood then how the dead and living meet: the living confer upon the dead a present moment, through our conscious attention, and the dead offer answers to the problems of the living by speaking unbound from existence or time.

This world is theirs, he thought. Theirs more than ours, because they're over and done but can return from any phase, whereas we have only this present, tiny moment, moving always and lost to itself, which has passed as soon as we take notice of it. The dead are more solid in this world than we.

Donna said: "Are you okay?" She was beside him, under the duvet. There was no transition between dreaming and awake. The seamlessness of it had disoriented him. He lay atop the bedclothes, still dressed, and in the darkness Donna's face seemed illuminated by a surreptitious light. He thought: It's never dark in dreams unless it's supposed to be, and it felt as if he still might be seeing what he should, and not — as in waking life — only what he could.

"I saw Mum and Dad," he murmured. "They told me things."

"You dreamt about them?"

"Not entirely. It was weird."

"You're not saying you saw them, like ghosts?"

"No. They're definitely dead."

"What's the difference?"

Big difference," said Steve. "Ghosts want attention. The dead come back only when we give it to them."

"Ever since you did whatever it was with Bailey, you don't seem able to stop thinking about them."

"I never left them, because they left me," Steve said. "I've never left anyone or anything, because I don't know how."

Donna put an arm around and kissed him. "Now that you know, you can move on, right? Maybe you should see a counsellor or somebody."

"I wish you'd been there when I lost them," Steve said. "You'd understand, if you'd met them."

"I understand you," said Donna, "because I know you. Your past doesn't own you."

"No," agreed Steve, "but I need to try and own it — except, I don't know what that means. The dead are lucky; they own the past because they are it."

"Now you're worrying me," frowned Donna.

trauma

Between your dreams and conscious thoughts lies reverie. It's unlike a daydream, whose ruling sign is story, and whose protagonist is the conscious ego. Reverie is cognition, but not narrative. A story tells you what you know already, although perhaps need to recognise. But falling into reverie — with luck — will help you to work something out, will present a solution, reveal something new. Thought, by nature, is rational — or so it's assumed — but reverie gives the lie to that. It's thinking, but with the rational safeguards turned off. It might be mistaken for fantasy, except the ruling sign of fantasy is desire. Reverie won't necessarily present you with what is hoped for or wanted. It meanders in unexpected directions and into undreamt-of places.

Down, thought Bailey, contemplating the goddess. *Down*, he thought, *down* ..., and his thinking took the shape of a snake, slid into a hole and sank, descending deeper as the reverie flexed and strengthened.

She, the goddess who none shall name, lived with her mother on earth but was abducted one day, taken down by the king of hell into his world of the dead. Imagine her horror of that darkness, when she was taken beneath the roots of trees, under the worms and burrowing creatures, into the dripping silence of caverns where light has never shone.

On earth, crops failed because the earth goddess was bereft of her daughter. What was essential to life had been forced underground. Even after hostage negotiations, when it had been agreed the goddess would return to her mother for a portion of the year, she never came back fully. The structure of reality was changed. She, upon whose mother's love depends all earthly life, had become the queen of the dead. Thereafter, for a certain period, life retreated each year into the realm of death, and death was found on earth. The goddess ruled over both and the intercourse between.

She was taken away. Abducted. Raped. The king of hell took her. His nature was to abide in subterranean realms, but it was not hers. She is greater than he, for she rules the dead and yet retains intimacy with the mysteries of life, and when she returns to earth it's with cognisance — not unlike a mortal woman — that into the embrace of death she must return.

Osiris, Baldur, Christ: the archetypal dying god. They're more familiar, perhaps. But she whom none shall name (for not even the king of hell commands her), she moves between the worlds yet does not die. What forced the linkage of life and death was her rape, the denial of her will and freedom. Yet her life remains the life of all: whereas by dying Christ saved the world, if the goddess dies it shall forever end.

No wonder then, thought Bailey, that in these times we feel her resurgence. The crops are dying. Plutocratic forces steal life from the earth, holding her to ransom. No wonder then, he thought, that she appeared, to tell me all I had would be taken. Our will is denied, but her life — the life of all — won't be taken while she abides in the world of the dead.

I'm not alone in sensing her, he thought. It seemed there were two ways to find her. The alternative to the route he'd taken was the path of the goddess herself: abduction, rape, trauma. When terror or violence rips a person from their world, what remains is a functioning shell. The living soul descends into the world of the dead where the goddess watches over it, and where it might remain forever unless descent is made to retrieve it. We may choose to enter the underworld, or else we may be sent there, but the challenge is to find the exit.

So far, he'd navigated by intuition, and his method — the use of a secret to fashion a unique way down — he'd discovered through feeling alone. But he sensed there were other, knowable routes in and through, and they might offer maps to help keep to the path. The maps were myths. The myth of the goddess showed him there were at least two ways down. The path of the goddess — abduction, rape, sufferance — had a feminine aspect. The path he'd embarked on — forcing his way down — seemed relatively masculine but no less torturous and dark. It was a path of abandonment, rejection, neglect, and of forced separation from love, life, and soul. He was entering the underworld to retrieve what was missing, withheld, denied, whereas that other path — the feminine — was a strategy to keep alive what had been stolen from earth.

A myth is a narrative, and narrative is linear. It charts the track whereby things came to be and weren't otherwise. No detail of a myth is inconsequential; rather, contemplation of details unlocks comprehension of how reality was formed.

The goddess didn't lose her way and wander into hell; she was unwillingly taken. Likewise — Bailey saw — in these times, there's no unknowing stumbling into environmental crisis. The earth is being raped and we know it. The abduction wasn't a detail added for drama but a picture of reality. The goddess isn't incidentally female. The link she forms between underworld and earth is a product of sexual conflict, but condemnation of the king of hell for toxic masculinity would be mistaking necessity for a character flaw. Perhaps, thought Bailey, the myth shows that the sad fate of every living being is rape and abduction by death. Yet the alternative would be worse. If the king of hell had never forced the goddess into his domain, it would have remained the realm of the inanimate rather than of the dead.

In its deepest layers, the myth was showing how, without union of life and death, the cost of never dying was never to have been alive, and that the price of living is sex. Unwilling sex marked the goddess's entry into the underworld as, perhaps, everyone enters this world sexed, cast in the form of either female or male — or, more rarely, neither, but no less unwillingly.

Was it, wondered Bailey, the current times staining his interpretation? The earth is dying — or so we believe. The feminine is forced underground, traumatised and angry, while the masculine consents to taking the blame. Neither tolerates the other, nor itself, because when life is failing sex fails too. Gender, thought Bailey, is the shade of sex; the ghost of real difference, stigmatised and banished, driven into the underworld.

His phone rang and he saw it was Donna. He wondered if it were Steve ringing from her phone, but, no, it was Donna, calling because — she said — there was something she wanted to ask him and, if it were okay, she'd come down at the weekend in person.

"Right. Okay."

He'd been exploring inside so deeply he wasn't fully back, and so the conversation felt part of the reverie: as if it weren't only the arrangement of a meeting but a symbol of something. The place and time arranged, Donna said bye and Bailey was alone in his room. He should eat and come back properly into his body; although, in this state, it'd been easier to talk with Donna, feeling barely a need to say anything at all.

The floor and bed were littered with books off the shelves, opened at wherever a myth or story might offer a map for obtaining his way down. He was a functioning member of society. He worked, paid tax, bought stuff. Yet he had the opportunity, so why not do as he liked? The guilt came from how it might look to others, who might label immersion in the inner world as self-obsession. But that would assume the self is isolated; as if looking inward led to someplace outside reality, of no relevance to the world. The cultural imperative is ever towards the outer, he reflected. If scientific research decided that looking within himself were good for society, there would be no need to feel bad. But he did feel bad, because it wasn't good for what society wanted itself to be. He only knew that it was right.

Kristyn had washed. He knew as soon as he entered because there was no stink. He called out and there was no answer, but he could feel her presence in the lounge. Again, the charade of her pretending not to be expecting him. It happened nearly every time. Bailey supposed it created for her a sense of having something that could be interrupted, rather than acknowledging she was a prisoner to her own torpor, lying under a blanket in her dirty flat. Presumably there'd been visitors, however, because it wouldn't have been for his benefit that she'd taken a shower.

Her face — its scowling eyes — disembodied above the blanket, pale and floating against the threadbare cushions and her unloosed hair, triggered a stab of panic in his chest. *You can't ever leave, because you love me.*

But I don't, he thought. It's guilt.

"What's the matter?" she frowned.

In some way, every relationship is fucked-up. This thought helped him stave off some of the dread.

"Nothing," he said. "Who's been round? Someone has."

"A guy from a community project to help me with my laptop."

"Oh? What was he like?"

"Yeah. Helpful."

The chances of this guy making a play for Kristyn, Bailey guessed, were unfortunately small. Back in the day, it would've been different. When he'd first met her at university, Kristyn was a goth pixie, ethereally skinny with big grey eyes and dark hair rolling down to her waist. She laughed nervously whenever she spoke. If someone challenged or tried to impress her, she'd quieten and withdraw, but he'd discovered if he met her cautious playfulness with more of the same then a resonance was established. Back and forth between each other they passed a tempered enjoyment of each other, which wasn't seduction, because Kristyn, somehow, made the pleasure all about that moment, without regard to its leading anywhere.

Back then, not far removed from adolescence, to Bailey she seemed a faery who'd emerged from the forest, at any moment prone to retreat, but irresistibly drawn to the wilderness's edge and delighting anyone who found her there. He was younger then. Even so, years later, when they were together, that spell she could cast of enchanted innocence would subsume them both. In their early days as a couple, it was a glamour they cast over everyone in their orbit. What's more compelling than a love so strong it takes a form palpable in the eyes of others? That brief period was the only time he'd felt joined together with someone in something, rather than always trying — and usually failing — merely to connect.

The contents had rotted inside their container. What they were now was no less impossible to create without each other, but what held it together was dependency. Now, it could surprise him sometimes with so much dread that he'd just caught himself hoping some random guy would take Kristyn off his hands. He'd been younger back then, but still he should've chosen his metaphors more wisely: the woodland faery is never what she seems.

Because she never left the flat, if Bailey were outdoors then he was alone, and if he were indoors with Kristyn then they were alone together. He would not have imagined a relationship so proximate could be so lonely. Some might say there are no such things as relationships, only individuals projecting onto others feelings that are never genuinely shared, a worldview that suits the materialist who regards living beings as biological units, separate and apart. It made no sense to Bailey, who'd seen and been seen by beings without bodies; who'd lived through weird coincidences where reality had circled back upon itself — just for a moment — to smile and wink at him. Just because he was lonely, he didn't mistake the universe for a lonely place. It teemed with beings and souls. Relationship was no illusion but an environment in which endless variety flourished, because hate is a relationship, and ignorance too. Bailey's unhappiness he shared with millions, its cause not to do with absence at all, but presences of troubling kinds.

"You're quiet," said Kristyn.

"I'm working on something that's difficult to talk about," Bailey said.

"I don't have conversations anymore, because I can't meet people like I used to."

"I'll tell you about it if you want."

"Only if you want," she said. Clearly, she was angry before he'd even begun.

What he told her was barely anything, only a tiny part. He was noticing, more and more often, little details in stories that jarred, making either no sense or twisting the meaning in queer directions. In these anomalies he'd find a weird hook or foothold he could use to pull himself deeper down.

The archfiend Mephistopheles gives Faust, the magician, a key to access the realm of nameless goddesses known only as "the mothers." Entering their realm bestows on Faust the power to conjure animated forms which delight his audience: the Holy Roman Emperor and his Court. But these people neither see nor understand how Faust has procured their entertainment. He went into nothingness, the void, where even the demon Mephistopheles daren't and couldn't follow. Indeed, Mephistopheles wasn't certain that Faust would return. To meet the mothers demanded complete cessation of being, possibly forever. But, happily, Faust comes back and with his new powers manifests on stage Helen of Troy and the hero Paris, both reanimated from ancient days yet unwitting of their audience.

The women of the Court are overwhelmed by the manly beauty of Paris but see nothing special in Helen. Likewise, the men: enraptured by the charms of Helen, they observe nothing in Paris that seems better than themselves. Faust is not immune either: when Paris makes his move to seduce Helen, in a fit of jealousy Faust destroys the scene he risked non-existence to obtain, plunging the Court into darkness and tumult.

"I think Goethe's showing," said Bailey, "that even when we're confronted with a true miracle, we recognise only our own desire in it, or — if we can't find that — nothing at all."

"You're going to say Faust should've stayed in the void," said Kristyn.

"What makes you say that?"

"Because the show lures people into delusion. Except the whole point of this story seems to be that they would've had those delusions anyway. They know it's a show. They're there to enjoy it."

"Even if he wanted, Faust couldn't stay in the void. You can't be in the void," said Bailey.

"Think about it," said Kristyn, "Helen of Troy and Paris — the real thing; both of them in the flesh. If it weren't worth going into the void for that, what would be worth it?"

"What would you bring back from the void?" asked Bailey.

He doubted foremost on anyone's list these days would be characters from Greek mythology. When Goethe was writing, everyone would've known who Helen and Paris were and what they represented. Maybe they served the same function as present-day celebrities.

"I bring things from the void all of the time," said Kristyn. "The stuff I collect all comes from there."

He contemplated some of her latest acquisitions piled against the sofa, some of them still only partially unpacked: a wall clock, whose hands formed the moustache of Frida

Kahlo; a black diamante puppy with the legs and tail of a scorpion; a collection of tea trays emblazoned with the ident logos of 1970s television companies: Thames, London Weekend, Anglia.

"But what can you do with it all?" he said.

Sometimes, the longer we've known someone, the more fraught with risk conversation becomes. Bailey and Kristyn avoided talking because of how well they knew each other: the tender spots, triggers, and fault lines. Relationships can reach a point where even light conversation sends down shockwaves that shake the foundations. With Kristyn, Bailey was often aware of a phantom conversation going on inside himself, where things that couldn't be spoken afforded reminders of the true contours of their relationship. Real conversation is how people explore one another. The phantom conversation wasn't that, but offered a map of spaces that no longer existed.

"Don't tell me what to do. You always do that."

"That's not what I meant. Whatever we choose as an ideal, it'll prove disappointing somehow. That's all I meant."

"What I like and spend my money on has nothing to do with you."

She was spoiling for a fight, and anything he said would be the means to have one. She'd lured him in and then destroyed the conversation she'd pretended to want. These were her moves, and in this dance his would follow. In the phantom conversation, he heard himself saying: You make me bad so there's no badness in you, and she replied: Because I can never find goodness that outweighs it. Yet this remained only a picture, because the absence of that goodness gave them no basis for anything.

Bailey's move was what he always did and what Kristyn depended on him for: he disappeared. Briefly, there was a red-hot nugget of contempt. He was sick of her, of this, and longed to erase it. She saw it in his eyes, but knew she needn't fear him. Seeing that she saw, he looked away, hating himself now more than he hated her. He levitated above the searing coals of rage. Waters washed in and quenched them, then receded, leaving behind damp ashes in their backwash. A wind blew in, drying and scattering, until nothing was left.

If this were a spiritual faculty — equanimity, whatever — then he didn't know why it felt so wrong. He chose not to retaliate, but what he would assume was best didn't feel so. Something worse, he sensed, might be better. Peace is false when it's avoidance of a fight it would be better to have had. Exhaustion swept over him. How is the world always in contradiction? He would let go, disappear, and feel soon as if nothing had happened, continuing as before, but the sickness and anger would continue also, because disappearance lasted only until he returned to awareness. This was his way of coping with Kristyn, but it gave him no means for being with her.

Nothing was said. A wounded silence pervaded, a wordless gap, where the conflict continued inside them as separate, stifled resentments; and when, during the course of the afternoon, tentative small talk resumed, it was as desultory and excavated of intimacy as always.

Kristyn supposed Bailey would disparage Faust for returning from the void with fripperous illusions: not entirely illusions, because the actual Helen and Paris manifested, but how real is a couple whose bodies centuries ago turned to dust? The void is unambiguous, and Faust's creations provoke confusion, yet where else was there to return to except the physical world? The void isn't anywhere, but having been nowhere — the realm of the mothers — Faust returned with the power of creating illusion as if it were a gift the nameless goddesses conferred. What there is nothing becomes, here, anything. Are nothing and anything so unalike? The oddest part — thought Bailey — was Faust falling for his own illusion, triggered to rage and jealousy by Paris seducing Helen, for even though Faust knew it wasn't real his desire for unreality was.

This felt familiar. In Bailey's visions were experiences that left behind nothing but absence; a void beyond memory and understanding. Nothingness never lies, but it can't be brought back, and yet the descent and return are both futile unless something is brought back. If that can't be nothing then, maybe, at least it can be false. Whatever the goddess gave him, it might not protect or deliver, but would likely drive him deeper into the world.

hierophany

A city speaks in two voices: one contemporary, the other
ancestral. Maybe every place does the same, but in cities
the contrast is stronger, more paradoxical. Brighton spoke
to him goadingly through the price of property, rents, the
low levels of wages, the cost of items in the shops. Can you
afford your home? A question that drains motivation. No
one wants to work harder just to stay where they are.

Bailey heard this voice. Increasingly loudly it told him
that Brighton wanted rid of him and would do her best to
shake him off the hem of her skirt. But his knack for clinging derived from listening to that other, ancestral voice.

One windy day, up through woods he'd found the
summit of Whitehawk Hill, where the gale tore itself to
shreds through the metal frame of the transmitter tower. It
loomed up into the roiling clouds, a gigantic stick-figure
burdened with spears and drums. There was archaeological
evidence on the hill for neolithic winter solstice gatherings;
even without knowing that, he could feel the sky, land, and
sea intersecting here with a tight, ineffable focus. His gaze
and body were drawn to the eastern side of the summit
overlooking the turbid, slate-grey sea, but frustrated by the
transmitter building and allotments that blocked access to
where he sensed had been — and still was— the soul of the
place.

The immense muffling and baffling of wind through the steel of the tower buffeted his ears in a lost but urgent language, felt as much as heard, so that he wasn't sure if the sympathetic vibrations of awe in his belly were a physical reaction, or a communication. It was easy to picture how, in the dwindling light of the year's shortest days, the ancestors had lit great fires on the seaward side, having travelled for weeks to gather here, where the earth and the sea and the air were joined.

Up on the hill, the ancestral voice spoke with an elemental authority, whereas down in the city's flat, central valley, along the strip of narrow parks and open spaces that led towards the sea, it muttered and whispered. A mood both tense and dull pervaded the lawns of Victoria Gardens, a nondescript patch hemmed in on each side by clogged roads. This configuration of place and situation spoke a story — somehow — of misery and shame. Two stone plinths, lacking statues, inscriptions erased by grinding, were rumoured once to have hosted effigies of disgraced politicians, hanged for corruption. If untrue, the story agreed at least with the atmosphere and the times. To hear the ancestral voice was, Bailey knew, no guarantee of an uplift.

The ancestral voice is a trace of how a place served the dead, whereas the contemporary voice is the demand of place upon the living who have no option for survival other than to meet it, while the dead may tell at leisure their tale of how they didn't. These voices are not contradictory, but identical tellings from different perspectives. The angle of the dead mitigates the present, smoothes it out, with meanings unskewed by the clamour for advantage.

He'd walked to Whitehawk Hill that morning. The weather was mild; a subdued gleam on the sea from a pale sun hidden in vapour. Then he'd descended, and now he was skirting Victoria Gardens, heading for the café where he'd arranged to meet Donna, hopeful that a place where the ancestral voice spoke loudly would immure him from the contemporary, of which — it seemed to Bailey — Donna was a strident spokeswoman.

When she phoned she'd not said what she wanted to discuss, but of course it was Steve. There was nothing else she'd ask for or tolerate his opinion upon. He decided not to think about it in advance; whatever it was, Donna would carry out regardless. If he couldn't affect her decision, he could at least gain insight into what she was planning, because now that she and Steve were living together, he'd been half expecting some kind of *coup de grace*, some move to terminate his and Steve's friendship, which he'd always sensed she resented for reasons he couldn't fathom. Perhaps distaste for the occult. Maybe just jealousy.

It puzzled Bailey that she was coming down by car. Brighton was a nightmare for drivers. She couldn't expect him to entertain her for a whole day. Perhaps she had friends here — he knew so little about her beyond Steve. The conversation might be awkward. He couldn't share what he was thinking about and working on. Donna's conversation consisted of things she'd done or seen, which Bailey found taxing. Apart from how those things had made the person speaking feel, there's not much to extrapolate. Probing someone's perception of their experience can seem as if they're being treated like a liar. He was more comfortable with conversations about ideas, because nothing need be taken for granted, and rough handling of theories wounds no one. Yet he couldn't talk that way with everyone. If he described to Donna how he was exploring methods for meeting the goddess of the underworld, searching for ways to talk with her, except the goddess appeared to be waiting for him to die, then Donna, he knew, would be listening as to someone who'd discovered a new restaurant or returned from a cruise around the Norwegian fjords. "That sounds great!" would be the best he could hope for, but not what he would obtain.

If Donna's intention were warding him off from Steve, then he would listen agreeably — and defy her. Unless it came from Steve himself, she could fuck herself. The anger surprised him — more so, since he didn't really believe that this was what Donna had come for. He didn't know her well, but well enough to sense that, although she often had a stick up her arse, she wasn't spiteful. What he really felt was a wounded resentment. Digging deeper, he realised it was loneliness. Kristyn's horizons were closed so tightly he couldn't imagine her driving a whole morning to discuss her concerns about him with Steve. Unless they impinged immediately upon her, he doubted concerns for him would even arise.

A feeling of desperation hid behind his suspicion and irritation towards Donna. He opened up and gave it space to subside. Everything was okay. He mustn't confuse his feelings with the circumstances producing them. If only he weren't so good at loneliness. Maybe it would help to spend time getting to know Donna. It wasn't often he was out in public with someone.

When Bailey and Steve hung out, there were parts of their lives they didn't share. Friendship has a degree of reserve, which distinguishes it from an intimate relationship. In intimacy, everything that's special is shared whereas, in friendship, just as special is the holding back of certain parts. Bailey never spoke about his parents' divorce to Steve, partly from respect for the greater tragedy that Steve had endured, but also because of a darkness, difficult for

Bailey to put into words, which he knew was alien to Steve. There had been animosity and silence in the house where Bailey grew up which was never explained nor spoken; an atmosphere Bailey inhaled until it became a part of him, a wariness to trust things were how they seemed — especially in the case of anything that offered enjoyment. This solidified over years into an irreducible melancholy that Steve indulged, even though it was by nature something that he didn't understand. It formed a major contour in their friendship. But, between friends, such contours don't go unrecognised; they're fully felt, sometimes as a theme of jokes and jibes, but always quietly respected, and sooner the friendship might end than changes be demanded.

Maybe, thought Bailey, in getting to know Donna better more of the contours of him and Steve would come into view. Steve's attraction to Donna — to what Donna was, her way of being — was something that Bailey held in reserve for Steve as something he couldn't understand and — in the interests of friendship — refused the need to.

He'd arrived at the café, one of those ubiquitous chains, always busy, but he made out Donna at the back on a leather sofa the other half of which she'd reserved for him with her bag. She was engrossed in her phone and didn't notice him until he spoke.

"Well, this has never happened before," he said. She moved her bag and put her phone away. "You made it down in good time," he said, sitting.

"The M25 wasn't as bad as usual."

"Nice. Can I get you anything?"

"I'll get these," she insisted. "I wasn't even sure you'd want to meet."

"I was surprised when you called."

"I sensed I'd caught you at a good moment," she smiled.

She went to fetch the drinks. As she stood in line, she looked to Bailey more slumped and tired than he'd seen her before. She'd smiled, but her manner had been brisk, as if conveying there were things they needed to get down to.

"So," he said, and thanked her as she handed him his coffee, "what's up with Steve? There's got to be something, else you wouldn't have come."

Another smile. No mirth, but it signalled appreciation he was letting her get to the point.

"You two are working on something, but it's not going well for him. He's talking a lot about his parents and seems depressed. I thought all that was behind him, but now it's come back."

"Well, that sounds about right," said Bailey.

Donna regarded him. "It's not all right," she said. "It's affecting our relationship. Tell me what you're doing."

Bailey sighed. "It's a working to connect with our ancestors. We discovered that they're angry. To find out why — and hopefully put it right — we're going into the underworld to talk with the dead."

Donna clamped her jaw. Instead of what she wanted to say, she said: "Well, why are they angry?"

"I'm starting to think," Bailey said, choosing his words carefully, "it's because we're not helping them die properly. We don't seem able these days to accept people in the past for what they were. We judge them for not being who we think they should have been."

"If they're dead, who cares?"

"If the dead really didn't matter," said Bailey, "we wouldn't be talking about them. Evidently, they do matter, because there's still a connection between us and them."

"It's not having a good effect on Steve," she said, "and I don't think it's fair, because he has a lot of grief in his past. Whatever this is, it's hitting him a lot harder than you."

She wasn't meeting his gaze. It struck Bailey that her justified protest was diffused by uncertainty, as if she'd come intending to demonstrate anger, but something was distracting her.

"Steve knows what he's doing," said Bailey. "I've seen him handle worse."

"I don't think you've seen him like this," said Donna. "He's making mistakes at work. He spends most of his time on his own. When I go to see what he's doing, he's just lying there."

"Depression is the territory of this work. If he weren't in the dark, he wouldn't be making progress with it. Entering the underworld and depression are two descriptions of pretty much the same thing."

"No one knows what happens after we die," sighed Donna. "You don't. And if there's just nothing — which there probably is — then there's no point in any of what you're doing. It's play-acting."

"You're right: I don't know," said Bailey, "but tell me — what do you think happens?"

This wasn't the conversation he'd expected. It felt as if something needed to come to the surface. Obligingly, her gaze turned inwards. He watched as, unseeingly, she glanced left and right, searching not for words but reasons for putting into words what she was deliberating.

"I used to think there was nothing. Now I'm not sure."

"Something has happened, hasn't it?"

She looked at him fully for the first time. "Yes," she said, and couldn't believe she was going to tell him. On one level, it was so mundane, so circumstantial, she worried that when she'd put it into words, there'd be nothing to it, no substance. But another part was reluctant to open to him — to Bailey — which was ironic, given the utter nonsense she knew he and Steve believed in. If anyone would give a sympathetic hearing to what she was about to describe, it was this baggy, moon-faced bloke, so maybe she was troubled less by the thought of failing to convey the weirdness of what happened than by the prospect that she might.

It happened on the drive, before she'd reached the motorway. She'd been thinking how the story she'd told Steve — that friends had invited her out for a day's shopping — was, at best, a half-truth, but found herself comparing this to the lies she'd had to tell her ex: lies to protect herself from his reaction if she'd told the truth. If she gained more sense from Bailey than she'd extracted from Steve, then the lie she'd told would be worth it.

On a stretch of flat, single carriageway which twisted gently between patches of woodland and open fields, in a layby up ahead, a strange shape and movement had caught her eye. At first, it looked like a black plastic sack flapping in the breeze. But it had too much mass, and in the next moment it became clear this was no object moving randomly with the wind, but something struggling under its own volition to rise. Her insides clutched at the pained, fretful manner of its movement, and — without even deciding — she snapped on the indicators and slowed.

It resisted making any visual sense, even after she'd stepped from the car. But as she drew up close the glossy black undulations resolved into a pair of crows, sprawled together on the road. Neither showed signs of injury but were obviously dying, too weak even to muster escape as she squatted down to examine them.

They were so large: great big wings and curved black beaks, with fluffy heads and shaggy breasts that she wouldn't have expected close-up on a crow. She wondered if they might be ravens. They had quietened and now lay still, apart from rapid, shallow breaths that twitched their throat feathers. Their unseeing eyes seemed focused neither upon Donna nor each other.

Intermittently one would struggle to rise and weakly flapped its wings, which the other sensed and would begin struggling also.

Never had Donna watched anything die. Wild animals are seen alive, or dead, or perhaps sometimes in the process of being killed, but rarely in the act of dying. Yet both ravens were approaching death, for reasons she would never know. She couldn't help or save them. What held her in place, however, was a sense of obligation to these dying creatures that ordinarily would have passed away unseen. For most animals, their death is unwitnessed, whereas for a human to die alone and unnoticed seems a travesty. She knew nothing of ravens — was uncertain even that that's what they were — but if she'd not been present then their passing would've been like the mythical tree falling in the forest which makes no sound because no one's there to hear. An animal dies with no one knowing that it lived: is this "death?"

When they were children, Donna and her sister had cats and rabbits. Mum always carefully shielded the girls from the suffering at the end of the animals' lives. These great, shaggy ravens, feathers grey and dusty from the dirt of the road, were different, because animals that live with humans accrue a veneer of identity and their ending becomes like a human death: the conclusion of a story. These black and feathered beasts of sky and field were a mystery to Donna

— not in the shallow sense of being unknown, but in the failure of language to encapsulate their way of being, which was not human.

If consciousness is the conferral of qualities, and if — potentially, at least — it burns brightest in a human soul, then maybe she could do more than feel helpless; accomplish more, perhaps, than simple reflection on the commonality of the ravens' mortality and hers.

With each passing moment they grew weaker, their struggles briefer and spaced further apart. Had poison killed them? It didn't matter. The eyes of birds lack sentience yet have a vital brightness. The ravens' eyes were dull and grey. The life was retracting, and what had found expression in raven flesh was struggling for purchase, readying to dissipate. It was like nothing she'd felt before — nor would she have believed that she could feel it — but she was sinking with them, her sense of the world attenuating. She was squatted on the tarmac. The periodic swish of passing cars grew faint, and her field of vision, filled by the dying birds, felt as if it blocked out what she truly needed to see, as if it were an impediment to a sightless realm into which her mind was shifting. She was concealed by her car from passing traffic, or else the sight of a lone woman hunched over in a layby, hazard lights on, might have attracted attention. But this did not distract her, for she was absorbed in the ravens and the growing sensation of dissolving with them out of the world.

No motion, only breaths, shallower and shallower. The twitch of a taloned foot. The loosening of a beak. It wouldn't be long, and she had followed them down already into a state of such rich and complex silence that any notion of a return path was lost. The only route was deeper inwards.

Her gift to the ravens she gave freely. Their deaths would otherwise have been the unwitnessed ends of wild animals, but the human mind confers qualities, and so their passing had from her a shape and a mood. Fate had drawn the birds together. She sensed how the larger one was sinking more gratefully into death. The larger was the wiser, but the smaller bird loved life more and, although both were sunk beyond any chance of continuation, the smaller one, rather than looking forward at death was watching his life recede. There had been camaraderie; not from long acquaintance, but like the kind that's born on a battlefield. That's what Donna saw and knew, but how it translated into the lived experience of ravens, she did not know. All she could feel was feelings.

Then it dawned that she had reached her limit, beyond which she would no longer be giving what otherwise they wouldn't have had, but instead depriving them of what was theirs alone. Their way of being was not hers. They had to die the deaths of birds: creatures for whom the sky and air are no limit on the earth's extent; who possess means and paths for walking upon the weather; for whom the lift of the wind is an ever-present companion, unfailing in its love.

It was hard, but it was time to give the ravens back their dying, because although the human is linked with the animal, within that intimacy is also a great remove. The animal is always authentic, but in the human is capacity for levels of contradiction and disingenuousness. Donna had given the ravens awareness of their dying, but also of death having meaning. It wasn't necessary to the ravens to be witnessed, yet because she'd lent them her awareness something unnecessary had entered the world. What needn't be, but is, is the very definition of meaning.

The birds had ceased their movements. The breeze caressed their feathers. She drew herself up, got back into the car, and pulled out from the layby onto the road, watching the motionless black heap recede in the mirror.

What had happened didn't yet feel as if it were hers. This was Steve's territory. If she put the experience into words, it would sound like the kind of things he and Bailey talked about. She wasn't sure that this was supposed to have happened to her. Watching two birds die was the crassest description. Yet she'd pulled over and been led into realms she'd never have guessed at: stillness and silence, a closeness to death in the midst of everyday life. What troubled her, with a few miles now between her and the layby, was — she realised — anger. It enraged her that what she'd seen she could not unsee. There was no choice, no option, for undoing what she'd witnessed.

She'd supposed, until now, that magick was something a person believed in, or not, and — on balance — she'd supposed that she didn't. Some of Steve's belongings from his old house gave her the creeps: the Ouija board especially, and the amulets and charms that looked— well, evil. She would've preferred they weren't in the house, but without conceding they worked she had no grounds for protest. Steve could do his thing and she would do hers.

For weeks she'd had to cope with a depressed boyfriend, obsessing over parents who died years ago; a boyfriend who — most worryingly — had started to talk, in a veiled way, about having conversations with them. Never mind Ouija boards and amulets, the mood in the house was so thick with loneliness and dejection that ghosts may as well have been walking in and out through the walls. And now this: ravens — midnight-black birds of ill omen, of graveyards and battlefields. Since leading her to that silence on the edge of consciousness, death felt all around her and inside.

Surely, this was not coincidence. Anger rose again at the thought of those who'd elected reasonably not to believe becoming unwilling collateral damage to those that did. Whatever Steve and Bailey were doing, evidently it was affecting her too. She could taste it, and it had a flavour she knew too well: gaslighting, the fear of going crazy, because, on the one hand, all she'd noticed was two birds in a layby, but on the other she'd been summoned into the world of the dead. Maybe Steve and Bailey enjoyed the ambiguity. Maybe for them it made life more interesting, but to Donna it felt like manipulation. Her psycho ex had used confusion to control her. Knowing where she stood was enough of a challenge. Having to work that out with regard to things not even human? She could do without that.

Yet there was plenty about the experience that felt compelling — sharp, tiny hooks of meaning that had pierced her and couldn't be shaken loose. If it had been a person she'd found dying by the road, never would she have dreamt of leaving them, and if no help came she would've stayed until they died, and longer. But not only had it seemed permissible to leave two dying animals, it felt like the right and proper thing.

This was curious. For the remainder of the journey, she reasoned it out. If she were at the side of a dying person, she'd never have left unless they requested it, for if they requested it then she wouldn't be abandoning them, and if they couldn't make that request then it would seem kindest to assume she must stay. So, perhaps it was a question of fulfilling the person's wishes. It was inconceivable that a wild animal would want the presence of a human, although, maybe, a pet or domesticated animal might.

Maybe, she thought, that's what domestication means: the possibility for an animal to have wishes. If those weren't met, then it would indeed be neglect and abandonment. But a wild animal neither wishes nor needs a human presence, and what a wild creature never wanted it couldn't be neglected or abandoned by. In walking away she'd given the ravens back their deaths, and that was why it felt right. If they'd wished for or wanted her, then indeed it would've been abandonment. She'd not abandoned, but had consigned them to necessity because, in the absence of wishes, there's only that.

Thinking this way wasn't hard, but what it opened up were levels of participation she wasn't sure she wanted. Presumably, this was the point of it: on the one hand, choosing to read experience the way she always had, or else accepting the invitation to extend awareness into dimensions of meaning beyond the perceptible. If the latter, then things were obviously different there. Her agency was augmented, for if she intended something then that was tantamount to its already having happened; and if she thought, then that was an action. As she approached the outskirts of Brighton, there was no avoiding that this wasn't thinking in the way she'd understood it previously, but engagement in an action that changed the world. The ravens and these thoughts that she was having which they'd inspired, made a difference so palpable she felt entirely changed, and she could sense how the effects of it would change others also.

analogy

If the divine is thought of as being neither male nor female, then what's being expressed is something beyond human, something complete and lacking nothing, because only the divine has no other. God as non-binary captures a sense of its absolute freedom, its power, because humans must have bodies, but the divine is unlimited by physical conditions.

If the divine is imagined as male, it's a picture of a certain kind of relationship. Men are fathers, but can't carry a child to term or birth them. A male god's relationship to his creation — likewise — is paradoxically intimate and yet indirect. If he is looked for within his creation then the search ends inevitably in failure, and he must compensate for his absence with an extreme gesture of love.

Because they're different, the sexes are not equal. Expressing that difference, one or other may present itself as greater. But nothing is greater than the divine. No surprise, then, if sexual analogies prove sexist when deployed to convey the difference between human and divine nature. That is the point of using them.

If the divine is female, what's expressed is that which, from love, and regardless of pain, doesn't flinch from descending into the world. She is here. Always close.

She is reality. Nature. Manifestation. But proximity can be fulfilling or frustrating, depending on whether reality consummates desire or denies it. When the female divine takes on forms that suggest sexual promiscuity or chastity this says nothing about how women should or shouldn't behave. What's in play is the relationship to reality. She may be accommodating and available, or an impenetrable mystery — or maybe at the same time both.

Separation from the divine comes in different flavours also. The pain of the absence from god can take on the form of ways in which men or women hurt one another. Men use anger, violence, and control. Reality, in bad times — times of setback and trauma — attacks like a ruthless warlord. Women, however, to cause hurt use rejection, abandonment, shame. In times of insufficiency, when what's needed is withheld, the world acts like a neglectful mother, inflicting a no less destructive variety of hurt.

Donna, describing her meeting with the ravens, ignited in Bailey an amazement that gathered in intensity, growing in its scope as his understanding grew.

She had attended upon the deaths of two animals as, in his vision, the goddess had waited for him to die. Here was an analogy that embodied a primary axiom: as above, so below, because as Donna had been to the ravens, so the goddess was to Bailey. The hairs rose on his nape with a prickle of inspiration and wonder. As the woman to the animal, so the goddess to the man. Powerful magick, evidently leading somewhere.

In the vision he'd hit the limit of his understanding, but Donna's story lifted him past it. He was in the place of one of the dying ravens (Steve was the other, probably) but his vision had told him also that animals were brought together purposely in that subterranean space; brought together to encounter one another and have their natures changed. Donna had met two ravens and gifted their deaths with meaning. They in return had offered transformation, leading her into the world of the dead. His vision had described the shape and mechanism of Donna's encounter before it had happened.

Donna could see the effect of her narrative upon Bailey: he'd interrupted her not once, and his attention had grown more and more intense until, wholly unconsciously, he was hunched forwards, absorbed in every word, undrunk coffee turning cold, both of them wrapped fully in the other's gaze. As she watched her story working a transformation upon his understanding, so he saw how the experience had produced a change in her, a rift, still expanding, like a receding horizon within which she had yet to locate herself. To Bailey she seemed no longer the person he'd assumed he knew.

He sensed she was coming to terms with what she'd seen, and was unsure yet whether to settle for the habitual and mundane — always available as a speedy opt-out — or this improbable, bizarre, psychotic dimension of meaning the magick had unfurled. It was a dangerous moment for Donna, as she made her choice and took its consequences, and also for the relationship between them. He didn't doubt that she'd been caught in the backwash of his and Steve's magick. If she chose the opt-out now she might, rightly, be left feeling aggrieved. There was always the danger in magick of someone becoming, without consent, a means of manifestation. If Donna's experience became a message from the goddess to him alone, that would not sit well with Bailey, because Donna had not consented to act as his medium. She'd come for help with Steve, not to find herself enticed deeper into what she might choose to regard as madness. Yet, if she chose to accept the magick, then it had a facility — like nothing else — for providing a single means for many and diverse ends. Her experience with the ravens would have had its meaning for Bailey but, at the same time, a different one within herself, and both of them at once.

When she'd finished her narration, he told her about his vision of the goddess. He described, point by point, how what he'd seen there matched in analogy what Donna had experienced. It was a circumstance not often encountered: a story is told, and though the listener feels they know the story better than the teller, it's only through the teller's rendition that the listener realises what they understand. It isn't what a storyteller wants. No one likes to tell a tale the listener has heard before. But this is only an artistic concern. In moments like these, art rises beyond itself. Every film director wants to connect with the viewer, but when the viewer knows and understands better than the director — not because they've made the film but have lived it — then maybe the director is no longer an artist, but has become a magician, bringing into being what surpasses representation and becomes real.

"Well, okay," Donna said, when Bailey had finished. "Suppose my experience and yours line up: who is this 'goddess' and what does she want?"

"As she was to me," said Bailey, "you were to the ravens. In the layby, what did you want?"

"I needed them to know they were seen," she answered. "I wanted their lives to have meaning, so they would know they'd had lives worth living. But, in the end, I wanted to give them back their deaths, so they could die in the right way."

"You came so they would see their lives correctly," said Bailey, "and you abandoned them so they could die properly."

"I suppose so."

"There it is," said Bailey. "Thank you."

"It's not as if I felt like I was her. All I want is to help Steve, but I don't see how this does."

"I don't know either," said Bailey.

Understandable that she would bring it back to Steve. It struck him then how Donna never asked after Kristyn. He assumed Steve had told Donna about her. His heart sank. He realised, with a pang of guilt, that thinking of Kristyn had caused his heart to sink because it was so much more pleasant spending time with Donna.

He was suddenly self-conscious of enjoying Donna's company. She was Steve's partner, so neither he nor she had anything to worry about. But he'd viewed Donna always as a challenge to his and Steve's friendship, rather than seeing her for who she was: someone he could be friends with.

She was attractive, he supposed, in a homely kind of way. She'd be offended at being described like that, he knew. Whenever she spoke of Steve it was with care and affection. How good she is for Steve, he thought, and realised it was the first time he'd ever imagined Donna and Steve as good together. Contrary to expectation, she hadn't shut down the magical implications of her experience — not yet, anyway. She was someone who could change and grow and wasn't locked in denial: that's what Steve had found in her. He was lucky. Yet Bailey sensed how Steve tended to hide behind Donna, as his way of keeping one foot in the mainstream world. Maybe Steve imagined that this was always where he would find her. Patently, that wasn't who she was. Bailey wondered if Steve underestimated her.

Donna noticed Bailey was distracted. "What's up?" she asked. He blushed, and seemed confused, which, somehow, gratified her. Before, Bailey had always struck her as arrogant, aloof, but today he'd given her his attention completely, and hadn't insisted or preached at her about anything.

"I was thinking there's a way of being," he said, "that's living in two worlds at once. We've both tasted it." (He was relieved to deviate from where his actual thoughts had been flowing.) "In that way of being we feel the timelessness of the ancient myths."

In everyday life, meaning quite possibly seems fragile, or sometimes appears lost, as if meaninglessness were a real and separate thing, rather than what it is: just more meaning, the meaningful sense of meaning's absence. The loss of meaning is nothing a human soul ever needs to fear, because human experience is by nature meaningful. When the consensus insists that meaning exists nowhere apart from the brain, it may be useful to remind ourselves that the brain is real, and so reality itself is the source of meaning.

Bailey was living a myth. He knew it. The myth of the discontented man searching for his heart's desire. Each time it's found, it proves to be a poison. Exactly what he dreaded. It's a variant on the tale of King Midas, except the fateful contact produced not gold but faeces because, deep down, Bailey believed that whatever he touched would turn to shit.

But being lumbered with a gloomy myth, Bailey reasoned, is maybe not the curse it seems. It's like the story arc of a television series: all sorts of things happen in the process of the myth's unfolding, and all of it belongs only to this world, the temporary and conditional world, rather than that other, timeless place. It's only the surface you see, never the underlying story arc. So, it's very much the case, thought Bailey, that we should consider Sisyphus happy — and Tantalus, Ixion, and Prometheus. Because people are living out these myths visibly all around us, and even in the act of doing so they can appear radiantly contented.

"I'm not sure I want to live that way," said Donna, "although I think you're saying it's like that regardless."

Bailey wondered what myth Donna was living. Steve had told him about her absent dad and her abusive ex. Bailey had sensed the coldness between his own parents, years before they parted. Maybe it played its part in his need to make relationships work that never could. Maybe he and Donna were alike: she, recreating her absent father through relationships with men who never saw her. It would be hard work making an abusive psycho out of Steve, thought Bailey. Here she was, seeking help with the separation while Steve journeyed through the underworld. Maybe Donna is a variant on Echo, he wondered, invisible to a whole line of stand-ins for Narcissus.

"I'm doing this thing at the moment," he said, "where I assume a myth is the most meaningful expression of something, and every tiny detail must be considered as loaded with significance."

"Okay," said Donna.

"If there's an odd detail, or an event that seems strange, then these are apertures that open into spaces filled with meaning otherwise unimagined. You work with kids, don't you?"

She nodded, warily.

"Maybe you can tell me this ..." he said, and described how, after the goddess was abducted by the king of the underworld, the mother of the goddess searched for her desperately. Having ascertained her daughter's fate, in grief she disguised herself as an old woman, wandered about the human world for a while, and in the household of Celeus at Eleusis became a nursemaid to his infant son, Demophon.

"Why?" asked Bailey. "She's grieving. She's searching for her abducted, adult daughter. But then she decides to be a nursemaid to a mortal, male baby."

"Driven mad by loss?" said Donna.

When gods are brought low, it's into the human realm they descend. In the myth, the mother goddess, every night while the household slept, worked at turning into a god the infant in her care, Demophon, by placing him in the blazing fireplace. And he would've become divine, if only his mother, Metaneira, hadn't pulled him out in horror, having happened accidentally upon the batty old woman basting her son in the flames. The mother goddess was enraged by Metaneira's ignorance and ingratitude.

At this point, the myth fragments into broken pieces. In one version, the mother goddess prophesies that Demophon — now doomed to be mortal — will be killed in battle once he is grown. In another version, the interruption of the ritual immediately kills the infant and, in recompense, the mother goddess gifts his brother, Triptolemus, with the secret of agriculture. Subsequently, funeral games are held each year in honour of baby Demophon.

Either way, it's a mess. A debacle. And then the mother goddess, sick of slumming it in a human form, unveils her divinity and demands construction of a temple. The good people of Eleusis subserviently comply. Into her new temple the mother goddess withdraws, and there she broods, grieving her daughter, destroying the harvest out of pique until famine descends and Zeus is obliged to intervene.

A sinkhole in reality had opened. The goddess was forcibly taken down, and up above everything reeled and teetered, subsiding until the structure found its level once more through the deal, brokered by Hermes, that the goddess could live a portion of the year with her mother. For a human woman this would've been an odd arrangement: one foot in marriage, the other in childhood, but it was all a compromise to ameliorate a blatant act of violence, so small wonder if the consequences were strange and skewed. The goddess never went willingly to the underworld; it came and claimed her to be its queen. Something in the heart of reality is rotten when deities are forced to preside over realms of being not naturally theirs. Baby Demophon was collateral damage. Simply by reacting as a mother, Metaneira ensured his death, yet she was blameless.

Thoughtlessly raising up to divinity a mortal child, after her own divine child was rudely taken down, the crazy dabbling of the mother goddess was the problem. But she was hiding in a human form to mourn her daughter, because no other god would willingly set right the wrong Hades had committed. The abduction of the goddess broke reality, and it has never been entirely fixed.

"You don't raise a child by making them a god," said Donna. "Kids who haven't been taught that the rules of the world apply to them will struggle to cope as adults. We try to encourage them to think of others, and eventually they learn. This 'mother goddess' seems angry at humans for being human. I'm with Metaneira."

"Me too," said Bailey. "Kids need to learn how to be in the world, rather than being given ways to escape it. Not that either of us has kids," he added.

"I can see why you do this," she said. "It leads to interesting places, even though these stories are thousands of years old and probably never happened."

"Funny," said Bailey, "how the mother goddess, in her grief, tried to rescue Demophon from his mortality, but it all went wrong. Yet the goddess, as we've both experienced — you more directly than me — she gives us back our deaths so we can die properly. Like the kids you work with, it's as if being the right way, true to our human nature, takes us deeper into the other world than if we deny our nature by trying to be like gods."

Bailey could guess what a scholar would make of their conversation: subjective interpretation of mistranslated texts ripped from their context and distorted across rifts of culture and epoch. Layer upon layer of distortion. Yet suppose the human relationship to truth were like a hologram. Every tiny part is a picture of the whole, albeit miniscule. Cut a hologram through its middle and the result is not two halves but two smaller versions of the original. What if rifts in the truth made divides like that? If myth, as Bailey supposed, were meaning highly concentrated, then even if it were ground to powder, every speck would retain its salience.

"Well," said Donna.

"Yes," sighed Bailey.

"I suppose I had better make a move," she said.

"Thanks for your help with Demophon," he said. "I get it now: it's about how wrong things would've been without the deal for the goddess's partial return. The mother would've gone on trying to fix things, but not in a way that human beings can be fixed. Her daughter's approach is very different."

"I won't deny it's been weird," said Donna.

"You're in it too," said Bailey, "if you want to be."

"Is it really my choice?"

"In a dream we get to decide sometimes whether we wake up or go on dreaming, but we don't decide what delivers us to that point. It's like that, I think."

"What are you doing for the rest of the day?" asked Donna.

"Chores. Then I'll probably visit a friend."

"Kristyn?"

"Yes," said Bailey.

"Your ex, isn't she? Steve wasn't sure if you were still seeing each other."

"Steve's pretty up-to-date on the situation," Bailey smiled.

"Okay then," said Donna.

She seemed to be waiting, so he leant and kissed her cheek. Instead of returning the kiss she touched his shoulder. "Don't be a stranger," she said. "Come and see us both whenever you like."

"Thank you," he said.

Driving home, Donna reflected how the newness of it had, in part, made the meeting with Bailey significant. Her ex had had no friends. He drank with people from work she never met. When she spent what seemed to him too much time with her friends, there was trouble. She never brought them home. They knew some of how he'd behaved and, because they were her friends, they hated him for it. Talking about him with her friends hadn't always been helpful, but only a way to cope, which had maybe held her in stasis for too long. It wasn't quite the same, but she could tell that Bailey knew the recalcitrant shame that came from being in a relationship he couldn't display to his friends. He'd shut her down when she'd asked after Kristyn. She didn't have that problem now with Steve. A new set of problems, maybe, but better ones, she hoped.

Yes, it had done some good talking to Bailey. She felt more grateful for the way things were. Bailey had mentioned that Steve had dealt with worse in the past. He knew certain parts of Steve better than she did, and this reassured her. Steve having friends who knew more about him than she did: it was one of those new, better problems. She'd felt jealous; resentful of the past he shared with Bailey. It was sweet of Bailey to say she could be part of it, but she wouldn't intrude on that. He'd made the offer, which was the important thing. Her ex had limited her to only himself and had fooled her into believing this was love. It had made life simpler, which, at the time, had its attractions but, she reflected, as she descended a slip road onto the motorway, some parts of Steve she alone knew. His friends were not taking him away from her; they were making visible parts of Steve that otherwise she wouldn't see. Being friends with his friends was a way to know Steve better and, although there had been awkward moments, she and Bailey had made a good start. Besides, she thought, if a person doesn't click with their partner's friends, does it matter? She smiled, recollecting occasions when she hadn't liked a friend's partner. That was more serious.

It was not until she'd reached the stretch of road with the layby, passing it this time from the other side, that the outer world took command of her attention and, as safely as she could, she craned over, looking for any trace of feathered wreckage. In seconds, the patch of vergeside had sped towards her and receded, but she saw nothing except bare asphalt.

She doubted the birds had survived, or that they could've hauled themselves away to die elsewhere. Someone had intervened, possibly, or — most likely — a fox or something had carried them off already. That was nature.

Disappointment arose — the feeling of reality falling short of its appearance. The birds were gone as if they'd never been, but they really had been there, and that would never change. Their disappearance took away nothing, because they'd been real. This wasn't stage magic, where a dove is concealed and is revealed or disappears. In real magick nothing is hidden, but by altering reality itself things appear or vanish. It's not a trick or illusion when no appearance is created, but instead there's a direct alteration to what's actual. The disappointment — she realised — was not with the world but with herself. She was disappointed that she hadn't been more changed.

There was something further, something indefinable, which she could feel but not put into words. Either her life would go back to exactly what it had been, or else she would take a different view — and maybe end up sounding like Steve and Bailey. Yet, she sensed, even that wasn't as far as it could go, but only a return to the same kind of life with a different perspective. Whatever it was that now felt possible, however it might transform her, she guessed she probably wouldn't ever shake this feeling of not living up to it.

mimesis

The sun would go down, and the sound of the radio station would change. Its music would attenuate, fade, then grow back in strength, tracing a slow and unceasing, undulating wave. Alongside, distant voices sang in unknown languages, licensed by the planet's transition into darkness.

Listening to nighttime radio makes audible the physical impact of the dark. Digital technologies are immured against it: imagine if people at night appeared on social media who didn't exist in daytime; or companies and services, oddly changed, took over in the evenings from their daytime versions; or everything on the internet after ten p.m. were just weirder, less trustworthy. Perhaps this offers a digital metaphor of how consciousness at night is altered.

Bailey woke in the small hours, alone at home, with a feeling that something evil was close. No other words described it. He'd dreamt of a malignant presence. Jolted awake, he lay in darkness, tingling with a rising swell of fear, and he realised that neither sleeping nor waking had released him from it. The only remaining option was to confront it.

The house and the street were silent. A breeze blustered along the terrace as if it had waited for him, stirring the bushes and shrubs in gardens, rattling fences and windchimes, before abandoning him again to silence.

He lay and listened.

The feeling of evil was tangible, yet unmanifest in anything seen or heard. Better, perhaps, if it had been perceptible, for then it would've had a locus and a limit. Desperation took root in him on thinking this and realising how this is a world in which evil subsists — even though it abides in nothing. He must be very low down, surely, so very low down as to be lost at the utmost bottom of things, to have to live in a world where malignancy could afflict him without having to assume a basis in anything.

He was on the precincts of panic. The nearness of something bad, the fear, and an escalating desperation for release from what was inescapable: these were factors of an anxiety attack which, if he fell into the trap of trying to control it (an endeavour bound to fail) would quickly overwhelm him into blindly chasing the illusion of an exit.

As ever, the trick was an inward turn to focus on the feeling triggering the need to escape — which might transform from a longing for breakout into a possibility of ingress. It was unplanned, but he found that instinctively he was going down. He would take the evil, whatever its source, and ride it down into the underworld, taking it to the goddess.

The proximity of badness inspires dread, the encroachment of what's unwanted, and its intensity is proportional to the sense of its inevitability. He felt this, and it grew as he tuned into the formless evil: nowhere except close, and nothing but bad. Combining this with his usual technique of the secret no one knew, and the pledge never willingly to re-emerge, he descended, sinking and sinking, by means of a path so unique and convoluted that even should he try to break his oath return would be impossible.

The dread intensified, but its significance shifted, in a way that — he was shocked to discover — made him want more. Dread that's wanted is desired, and here he confronted the weird intersection of desire and dread. One is the ardent wish that what's present were gone, the other is passionate longing for what's absent to arrive. In both, the object is all-important: either what's to be avoided above all else, or wanted more than anything. This, he realised, was precisely his relationship with the goddess, she who waited tenderly for him to die: desirable for her compassionate ministration, yet dreadful because, to meet her, he must pass through death.

It was a blessing, the dread, because the proximity of evil betokened the goddess's presence on its other side. What appeared in this world as evil was, in eternity, her. This was true, but he felt it rather than understood. If he described the sensations he felt, this was a common-or-garden panic attack. He'd experienced a few. Steve sometimes had them, too. But Bailey had found a use for them: the symptoms led to the goddess. Panic attacks are widespread and, as an impediment to everyday activities, are a mental health concern, but as entrances to the underworld they were — Bailey mused — perhaps overlooked. Rather than a psychological weakness or a personal failing, they might be signals of love from the other side of death, which a journey through the underworld could obtain, a venture not without risk, and never lightly to be recommended.

The intersection of desire and dread was delivering him surely into the world of the dead. It had a visual analogue: moonlight. The light of the moon is bright yet passes through the dark without displacing it. Moonlight is brilliance and darkness, both at once. This was not a thought: he lay on his mattress with closed eyes and saw it. Watching the visual field with eyelids shut is, like moonlight, a seeing by means of a light that penetrates yet does not dissipate the dark. To call on the goddess he need only close his eyes and see. The light was milky blue and of the moon, for she was both the moon and the light in the eternal darkness of the underworld.

When unsure, a useful means to determine whether an experience is a dream is to locate a light switch and flip it on. In the waking world the room will flood with light, but in a dream — a lucid dream, for if the decision were taken to make this experiment, then the dreamer is conscious — something bizarre occurs. Bailey had encountered different varieties: the light switch transforming from hard plastic to the pliancy of flesh, intended seemingly to startle him awake rather than assist in attaining awareness within the dream; or else, light emerges from the bulb, but like a gel or liquid, possessing the colour of light rather than its luminosity as it spreads gradually to fill the room. Whatever the specific outcome, a confrontation with an anomaly was the trigger that might afford awakening within the dream.

Something similar applies to all so-called "methods" in magick: their efficacy, though unrecognisable to science, nonetheless offers consistency. Bailey understood that all his methods for obtaining the presence of the goddess might yield their result, but also that times would come when inevitably they would fail. It cannot be said that magical methods "work," for if they provided predictable results there'd be no growth nor awakening, as in a dream lucidity comes from noticing what's wrong or strange.

Reliable magick is merely technology. It's only when methods fall short that there's growth in understanding: this is the Great Work. From a materialist perspective, utilising methods bound to fail is madness — which, indeed, it is, for madness is the collapse of extant structures under pressure (pending growth or transcendence). Madness and magick are analogous. Good magical methods offer productive forms of insanity; their efficacy paradoxically consists in proving unreliable.

His most recent attempts to find the goddess yielded no more than what he'd arrived at before: the interminable silence of her waiting for him to die. The divine has infinite patience, but Bailey had not and was dogged by frustration and despair. The greater part of psychospiritual development is enduring the unbearable. Only when the intolerable is accepted does the breakthrough come, but recognising this confers no shortcut. Acceptance and understanding are alike, and just as a faked understanding will prove unsustainable, so anything other than authentic acceptance avails nothing. Genuine acceptance is love. Ultimately, love of the divine, passion for truth, makes possible a disregard of self when, in all its wrongness, the world is seen and longed-for regardless. This is the reason the biblical commandment to love god is placed above all others: it's fundamental as a means of gaining understanding, but repugnant when we wrongly suppose the divine demands this of us for its benefit.

Bailey had discovered the goddess waits for him to die. For all he knew, he might have to suffer this until his death. But then Donna had come with her tale of the ravens, offering an analogy that deepened their understanding — Donna, his best friend's partner, for whom it seemed he was developing inconvenient feelings. He had woken to a sense of evil and panic and discovered how dread was a vehicle. And now, although none of this was what he'd asked for nor how he would've liked it (it seemed so weird and broken, so quotidian, like an obsession or psychosis), because he hadn't chosen this and could never have conceived of it, he wanted, loved, and accepted it.

The goddess was here. He saw nothing, but in the silence of his room where the evil presence had been, now she was. The dread of what he hadn't wanted became the relief of having what was come. She might wait and communicate nothing, but Bailey didn't mind; nothing forever was perfect.

Transcendence must be abandoned, she said.

He reeled in surprise at the break in her silence.

There is no transcendence, she said.

He sensed she'd presently show him what this meant. In every awakening is understanding, but also a seed, a mystery, that betokens the awakened comprehension's latest limit. The ravens, Donna, and the panic attack had furnished enough death to satisfy the goddess he'd died, but even as he grappled with this a new horizon presented itself, over which — she seemed to be showing him — lay nothing.

The internal moonlight, that milky-blue luminosity which shone through darkness without displacing it, an image of darkness visible, had led him to a state never available before, although perhaps it was the same place where memory had previously failed and he'd brought back blanks. From here he saw how every event or happening, each experience, was equivalent with every other.

Equanimity is when the mind turns with welcoming readiness to whatever presents, whether it's painful or pleasant, annoying or dull. But this new state had harder edges, because the equality of experiences proceeded not from the mind's attitude towards them, but palpably, perceptually, from the experiences themselves. They didn't feel or appear the same, they were the same.

It was curious to proceed moment by moment when every moment was the same and also every experience within each moment. It didn't feel like being alive because now that everything happening was the same he wasn't within time. Things continued to unfold, but nothing was happening, because whatever came along was synonymous with what went before.

The meaning of things had also become strange. With everything the same, symbolisation stopped: there was no difference between signs, nor between the sign and what it represented. Bailey realised there was no possibility of magick here, but — because there was no difference between his will and reality — it wasn't clear if this weren't the apogee of magick — of magick raised to an infinite power.

He recognised it as what he'd talked about in principle with Donna but was now experiencing directly: living mythically. Gone was the appearance that the meaning or quality of a successive moment could veer into difference from its antecedent. 3:57 read the bedside clock, and it would cycle today through all the minutes and hours, displaying them in faithful sequence, but Bailey had penetrated the illusion of difference between moments and had seen the nature of experience as uniform: something that never happened, yet which is always happening. The stories of our lives, he realised, are stories about life itself. Everything that happens is a myth.

By presenting him with a gift, the goddess led him deeper: a circular shield of burnished wood, silver boss and edging engraved exquisitely with a Celtic knot pattern. Silver borders radiating from the boss divided its outward face into quarters coloured blue, red, green, and yellow. The design couldn't have been simpler, nor more perfect, but in this state of absolute equivalence the gift presented Bailey with a conundrum.

Recalcitrance is the usual relationship between self and world. What self desires is often not what's to be found, so it seems the world provides reluctantly. But a gift subverts the mundane — the best is given freely with no demand for effort or reciprocation. When each moment is equal, without a difference between experiences of self or world, there is neither gift, nor gratitude, nor deprivation. To demonstrate this, the goddess cast out Bailey into symbolic awareness where, immediately, he recognised the shield as a mandala, a symbol for the self. Her gracious bestowal of it was an undeserved gift originating from the other world, the transcendental realm. As soon as he'd understood, she drew him back into consciousness of absolute equivalence, and again: there was no gift and no transcendence. It was not a vision, and neither was it magick.

The goddess showed him a stone. *It has no soul*, she said, *no intelligence, no life.* He grasped what this meant: the stone was not a symbol; it was the non-symbolic experience of equivalence.

The path is made of stones, the goddess explained.

She meant that every stone on the path was the self. Every stone was equivalent to every other stone. This was not symbolic either, because there was no difference between one stone on the path and another, nor between what she described and what he experienced.

His sense of her had changed. The night was silent and her presence intense. He saw and heard nothing, but whereas formerly he would've described her location relative to himself as "everywhere but nowhere," now — it was odd and difficult to verbalise — she seemed somewhere.

Not here. Not in the room. But somewhere in the world. No longer in nothingness, nor in some transcendent realm.

It was strange and unlike how he'd ever experienced divinity before, yet still she was the goddess of the underworld. It was not as if she'd become a woman, living somewhere, who he might find, showing up on her doorstep one day, having tracked her down to an unassuming rental property on the outskirts of Aberdeen. No, her nature was still not of the world. She remained apophatic, except, retaining her nature of being apart from it, she was nonetheless within it.

A few days would pass before Bailey grasped what this was: the goddess was queen of the underworld for a portion of the year, but for the remainder she returned to her mother, the earth. Absent for the dark part, in the light she comes back. This shift, he realised, is the mystery of metaphysical summer. The state of being wherein there is no transcendence and no magick, where every experience is equivalent to every other, and each is a stone on the path and each stone is the self — this is the metaphysical summer, for summer comes when the goddess is in the world.

It was too much. When overladen with meaning, subjective experience becomes indistinguishable from reality and cannot be thought about but only lived as ecstasy, madness, truth, love, or some wild hybrid of all of these. The shield she had bestowed was no gift, but a given, because it was both the self and the creation, and these were his already — which was what she wanted him to know. It was like the shield of Achilles which, in Homer's *Iliad*, is ornamented all over with engravery depicting scenes of the Greek universe in microcosm. And it was like that ambiguous accoutrement of western magick: the pantacle — which some aver is merely a variant spelling of "pentacle" — but both pentacle and pantacle are means for showing in miniature what's at once the entirety of creation and the integrity of the self.

The experience faded, and that word "experience" became the only one he had for what had been unlike any previous vision. When every moment is equivalent there's no going in or out of vision, nor of any other state. Never before had magick led him into realms so contradictory of what he'd supposed "magick" meant. Perhaps that other world — the real, true world — can be approached closely enough that the phenomenal, the figurative, wears thin and the noumenal, the absolutely literal, is tasted for a while.

Her dual residence in hell and on earth is the special quality of the goddess. She affects reality by her departure and by her return. She rules the dead— the underworld shades who are shells, empty remnants of once-living souls — that while they cling to dim half-life are the least that humans can be. Yet the metaphysical summer of her return is another dimension of being human where the self is recognisable as synonymous with creation. Unconscious of this, human beings on earth live like the shades in hell. To become conscious of it, the journey must be taken and the way down found to the goddess to ask it of her.

Outside Bailey's window the darkness was lifting. He heard the piping of the earliest birds. The state of everything being equal was already a strange memory. He was returned to a world where something could appear as if it were something else; where seeming was as possible as being, and everywhere was haunted by little, ghost-like semblances of truth, just as the underworld teems with shades, traces of what were once living souls. It occurred to him that, having made the commitment on each descent never to come back up, he'd been taken at his word. He saw now how the everyday world was the underworld, where people mistook the appearances of others and themselves for what they really were. All this time, without realising, he'd been living underground.

He'd not slept since noticing the clock at 3:57, and soon his day would start with less than five hours' sleep. He was due at the call centre by 8am for a morning shift on the employee helpline, and it would start as it always did: a flurry of callers unable to face the working day — because of anxiety from collapsing relationships, or bullying at the office, or impossible workloads, or past trauma. Shades in the underworld. All of us, lost souls, seeking ourselves but finding only figments of what we've been mistaken for. To suppose what the goddess had showed him offered a solution or escape was only more lost-soul thinking. She'd showed him how the underworld was home, but clinging like a shade to a semblance of life was no way to live. The dead have no business aspiring to life, for this, precisely, is the making of hell. But if knowing it makes life neither easier nor better, then he might question where the benefit lay in his devotion to the goddess. Devotion with a prior aim or object isn't love, and the benefit of loving must be the beloved's. What lover would want it otherwise? Either he loved the goddess for who and what she was, or he worshipped a false appearance that satisfied himself. She'd showed him this world was the underworld and, likewise, pretending that it wasn't could only perpetuate the shade-like false belief that fixing the unfixable would deliver the longed-for reward. Rather, to Bailey, it was looking as if he must understand what being a shade entailed. In myths, the shades complained and bemoaned their depleted faculties and status — as if they couldn't bear comparison of their dead selves with their former identity alive. They seemed never to get the hang of truly dying. Bailey wondered if the path to metaphysical summer lay in the dead understanding death. Perhaps in the underworld the equivalent to living well would be to die fully, which seemed more dignified than moping in the dark.

What the going down betokened could manifest in various registers — as a spiritual practice, but also in depression and stuckness, abandonment, loss, and bereavement. The goddess was like a mechanism, embedded in reality. Instead of a binary being there or not, she was the means for goodness to become mobile, to depart and return. If human life were lived entirely in the presence of goodness, or without it, then good could neither be recognised nor enjoyed. But, because a mechanism performs merely a causal function, a being is the better way to comprehend her, through a relationship with her rather than by explication. The moveability or conditionality of goodness is not a defect to be mended or accounted for, but a quality of reality to be understood — loved, in other words. Seeing the goddess raises the possibility of a conscious encounter, or else reminders of her may take on the unconscious forms of melancholia and meaninglessness, the chronic agonies of goodness gone away.

This, Bailey realised, was how it felt with Kristyn, and how it had felt to a greater or lesser degree in every relationship he'd had. The goddess was in the world — that's what he'd been shown — but he'd lived as if her unavailability was a problem to be remedied. Each relationship had seemed more distant and impossible than the last until, with Kristyn, it felt like nothing at all, a shade of intimacy. But the goddess was in the world, which meant there was nothing Bailey had to do to make her appear there. He had neither to mend nor make up for anything that wasn't her.

He had only to look and find her, or else she would appear, which was exactly what had happened. He'd looked and she'd helped him to see her. With Kristyn he was doing the opposite: trying — hoping — to make something appear or reappear that wasn't there.

Maybe in a similar way — by trying to recreate love from her father she'd never received — Donna had latched onto her psycho ex. Perhaps she and Bailey had something in common to discuss, but Donna had suffered more, perhaps, and Bailey hoped she'd broken her pattern forever now that she had found Steve. The goddess had shown Donna something too — the ravens, which, Bailey supposed, must on some level be himself and Steve. Two ravens in danger. Odin's ravens. Blearily, he reached for his phone. There was no chance now of sleep. He searched the names of Odin's ravens, and the translated passage from that Icelandic poem he couldn't remember, but whose solid, despairing rhythm he felt moving through his mind. Here it was: *Hugin and Munin fly each day over the spacious earth. I fear for Hugin, that he come not back, yet more anxious am I for Munin ….*

Odin is the speaker, and the names of his intelligence-gathering ravens, Hugin and Munin, mean, respectively, "Thought" and "Memory." Striking how, despite the powers of both in bringing Odin knowledge, he worries for them. Hugin — Thought — harbours a tendency to fly onwards and never return, because thought knows no spatial limits and leaves behind the world entirely if it chooses. A question of obedience, perhaps. Yet Odin worries even more for Munin — Memory — who's vulnerable for reasons unelaborated. Memory's a fragile thing, prone to loss, error, and distortion, but maybe it's the converse danger Odin fears: whereas the temptation of thought is venturing too far, the lure of memory is submersion in what's familiar, in home, and in the past. Munin's peril is the potential failure ever to achieve a motivation for escape.

Steve was locked in his past, Donna had said; preoccupied with memories and dreams of dead parents and his childhood home. If Steve were Munin that meant — Bailey realised — he was Hugin. Here was a warning: that he shouldn't fly too far, and Steve must abandon the nest. Odin's concern was to welcome back his ravens at the close of the day, but the goddess was working a different agenda. The equivalence of every experience is the death of both Thought and Memory: for Donna, in the ravens' dying moments, there was little to tell them apart. The goddess attends upon the death of all, and the knowledge she reveals is that this isn't the real world, but the world of shades. Thought and memory reveal much, but both are themselves things in this world — the reason, perhaps, why Odin is so anxious for them. Thought and memory belong to the world of the shades and convey knowledge of that underground world only, but if they "come not back" then maybe a different sort of knowledge obtains, the kind the goddess provides.

crisis

Donna seemed different. Steve couldn't find the exact description but, on the one hand, she seemed more tolerant, not asking so many questions nor challenging him when he talked about what he'd been thinking. On the other hand, she seemed more distant, less engaged.

It might be assumed that a relationship — the feelings of two people toward one another — is reducible to a pair of stories, one each in the mind of the persons concerned. In that case, he was perceiving Donna one way, or now in another, yet nothing in her necessarily was changed at all. Likewise, assumedly, nothing had happened in him to occasion the apparent change in her. But he knew that relationships, in truth, weren't stories. When something changes, it's felt by both, because the change has happened, it's real. It's more convenient to imagine that only perceptions have altered, because when changes in a relationship are contradictory or complex then it's easier to explain. Having explanations makes it feel as if what's happened has been dealt with, even when it hasn't.

Donna was being more tolerant, and she was less present. Neither her nor Steve's perceptions were wavering; the relationship had altered. Tolerance is a form of distance; antagonism is more intimate than giving a person space.

This was maybe why Steve didn't like the change. He would've preferred Donna to have remained how she'd been: sceptical, dubious. Her attitude towards his magick had a resistant mass, a gravity, around which he'd taken a reliable orbit, never crashing to earth nor yet spinning off into untethered space. It felt as if with this change had come a growing propensity to drift further off into the dark and empty reaches of the distance she was affording him. If she wouldn't challenge or question him, he could only take a wider berth. It brought to light for him how he'd placed on Donna a burden of opposition; he'd relied on their differences to ground him. Yet maybe it wasn't as simple as this either. He felt dimly there was something here he misunderstood. That urge to withdraw into the increased distance between them made him suspicious of this grounding, this gravity, that he'd been relying on Donna to provide, because looking to someone else for an inward capacity raised the question why he hadn't found it within himself.

Weeks were passing — to what end it seemed unclear. He went to work and earnt the money that kept it going. Everything that had to be paid for was, which meant the time left over could be his own, but who he was and where: these seemed difficult questions. At work, he sat before his screen and the things needing to be done were completed to his usual standard, but his mind was in a private place where none could follow — which wasn't the realm of his home life. It was the world of his past, the deep and defining past that transcended memory. What currently he lived for was the encounter with this source, the origin and essence of himself, which demanded an application of continuous and conscious maintenance.

Dreams or visions, there seemed no longer any difference; he was aware throughout. However, on returning to the perceptual world there were details — things he'd done, thought, or said — which weren't enough like himself to avoid doubts over whether this was truly consciousness and not a semblance.

Most nights he'd spend with Mum and Dad in the old house. He'd mastered now the knack of being with them in ways demanding nothing new from them, so there were no more of those grotesque behaviours the dead resort to when embarrassed by situations that oblige a live response other than a repetition of the past. Sustaining this required of Steve a lightness of attention. Gazing too directly at anything in this realm risked seeing right through it; instead, he'd learnt to synchronise with what otherwise would seem its substancelessness, lowering the frame rate of his attention to match the gelatinous frequencies of the dead. Nothing is lighter nor quicker than thought, but extended periods in his parents' company necessitated this intentional coagulation, otherwise it would be like shining a bright torch onto a cinema screen while the film is playing: the precious illusion is spoiled and lost.

The old house had become more to him than ever, even supposing somehow he were to live there again, because his surroundings in this realm were not limited to a particular moment. Things that hadn't co-existed now could. The lounge, which had transitioned through changes in decor down the years might wear elements of them all, or make division of itself and become several rooms from different eras; or sometimes it might contain a curated array of objects that never were together yet instilled a consistent mood. Strangely, most powerful of all were rooms and objects that never existed, but which, rather than evocative of an essential sense of home were instead evoked by it.

One night, over Mum's shoulder, on a long-forgotten sideboard appeared an ornament: an oil lamp, like the kind in fairytales that houses a djinni. Studded with false rubies and emeralds — lumps of coloured plastic — when lifted it was surprisingly light, made of tin, and seemed dented and tarnished on purpose to create a faux antique effect. Mum owned this in the seventies, Steve recalled, when they were popular, except even as the memory coalesced, he knew it was fake. Mum never had this, although she might've, and — more so — he felt she should've done. Even though it never existed, the tacky ornament captured an era, an aesthetic, and — a feeling that came flooding back to Steve — his childhood fascination with treasure. Between the plastic jewels, holes were cut into the tin, in star and crescent shapes, and from the interior came a smell of camphor.

Somehow it was right that the oldest and most personal impressions of childhood were conveyed by images of things that never were, and memories that never happened, because what's expressed through fiction transcends it. If this other realm to which he'd oriented himself were only a collection of personal memories, then it was finite and quickly would begin to repeat itself. But it was more, and inexhaustible, because it wasn't defined by his own experience, and its truth — of his childhood self; his origin and home — was expressible in unlimited ways. He could live here and discover it over and over again, differently forever.

The dead had been angry but now seemed reconciled. By entering and inhabiting their world he'd found a means of harmony with them. The solution was to take the dead wherever he went. The old house was gone and a new life with Donna beginning, but that needn't entail separation; rather, in these visions he could re-inhabit the past in a non-regressive way, because the past has a truth that can be re-combined in ever-original appearances of the same, which — as long as he didn't look at them hard enough to see straight through — would retain solidity for as long as he needed.

Bailey had phoned and was coming to stay at the weekend: their first sleep-over guest. Donna was fussing over the decoration in the spare room. Pointless, because Bailey wouldn't care, but Donna insisted they must have it finished. It was a displacement, Steve supposed, a way she could feel that she was making Bailey welcome, even though a disposal of any formality would best achieve that aim. The three of them, he mused, might make an awkward dynamic, but there was room, if need be, for he and Bailey to break out. Even if Bailey had nothing to talk about with Donna, he and Bailey had much to catch up on. What Bailey had mentioned on the phone suggested their explorations had diverged. It didn't sound to Steve as if Bailey had connected with the dead but, similarly, in previous undertakings they'd received different things and had argued over their interpretation, only to realise, in the fullness of time, that the discrepancy was in their seeing, in their perspectives, and not in what had been revealed.

Every occultist struggles with the impression that other occultists are doing it wrong — and that's okay, as long as each accepts they might be wrong also. Where two people doubt themselves and each other, friendship and alliance can be slow to form. The solution — which he and Bailey had found — was to bracket their opinions and personal lives. Between them it was accepted that intimate relationships, financial circumstances, political allegiances, hopes and fantasies — the kinds of things where commonality usually is a basis for connection — these were matters of little regard, likely to be overlooked by the other, and only raised with a concomitant acceptance of their being overlooked. The mundane matters less to an occultist, and friendship must be forged from what's impersonal, which seems a contradiction, but the mutual desire to relinquish the quotidian becomes the foundation for sharing.

It can be a volatile arrangement, because toxic patterns of relating can masquerade as something similar: eschewal of another's concerns not from shared idealism, but from selfishness. Some would prefer a friendship on impersonal terms not to solve the problem of common ground, but to avoid concession to another.

At a party once, Steve, talking with someone he'd only just met about meditation and the esoteric, was accused of solipsism. He'd never noticed before how, indeed — superficially — they looked alike, yet whereas for the solipsist nothing exists except the self, for the mystic, apart from the self, everything exists.

Given how close to occultism certain traits of solipsism or narcissism could appear, from the outside — he reckoned — his and Bailey's friendship would seem strange. If truth be told, he suspected Bailey was more comfortable with it than himself. Sometimes it seemed that Bailey had the better deal — in the area of relationships, for instance, because whereas Donna and himself were pretty visible, whatever Bailey had with Kristyn was a mystery. Without opportunity to understand it, Steve felt he was denied the means to properly know Bailey.

He'd met Kristyn only once. Bailey asked Steve to wait outside while he went inside her place, "Just to check that everything is okay," even though Steve had already heard him phone ahead, and the visit had been planned a week in advance. It was several minutes before Bailey re-emerged. "She's ready," he said.

The hallway was dingy and thanks to the weird build-up Bailey had given it, Steve's imagination had run already to Dickensian visions of a decayed madwoman enmired in detritus. The piles of junk littering their path did nothing to dispel this, nor Bailey's nervous smile as they picked their way through the miscellany towards whatever presence waited in the room beyond.

She lay on a sofa, under a blanket, with only her face visible upon a pillow of her hair — grey, like her eyes, which stared into his unblinkingly, and in a childlike voice: "Hello," she said.

"Lovely to meet you," said Steve.

With a flicker of annoyance, she glanced at Bailey.

"Kristyn's not feeling great," Bailey explained, "but she wanted to say hi."

"I really wanted to meet you," she said, "but I can never tell if I'll have the energy."

"Well," Steve found himself saying, "we can always meet some other time, when you feel better."

She looked pleased by this remark, even though it was absurd.

"One day when I'm feeling better. Yes," she said.

What unsettled Steve most was Bailey, who hadn't taken his gaze once from Kristyn, but seemed consumed by an attentiveness that was one part solicitation and the other part dread. It revealed a side of Bailey that Steve had never suspected. Normally, Bailey was dispassionate to a fault, but here he seemed adrift, as if deprived of something. The greatest puzzle was why Bailey might suppose that whatever was missing resided in a woman like Kristyn.

"I don't get many visitors," she said. "People maybe find it too much."

Steve demurred, but she wasn't wrong. The spaces between people are alive with a living field of meaning. Words spoken modulate the field. Cultural conditioning encourages us to dismiss or ignore this subliminal yet ever-perceptible dimension, but in the presence of someone like Kristyn it's difficult to deny, for she was palpably sucking that living field of interaction into herself. Steve's visit wasn't a meeting; what was happening, she'd decreed, wasn't happening, and then she'd enlisted his collusion in this negation by obliging him to say that it was okay. What he really felt was a vertiginous chasm between them, into which all the life was draining.

Steve had an image of Bailey's relationship with her: as when a spaceship skirts a black hole's gravitational field, desirous of approach, yet wary of crossing the event horizon, knowing the fearful risk, because it's uncertain how far the horizon extends — so, Steve sensed, Bailey lived day to day in empty space, pushed out by Kristyn, but mindful of destruction if he drew too close.

He'd crossed paths before with people like Kristyn about whom the imaginal proved an effective forewarning. Their outward appearances — sometimes charming, or even seductive in a particular kind of dirty and dangerous way — were preliminary signals of the toxicity that lay in wait. Dickens's Miss Havisham, in her rotting bridal dress, was a translation into physical perception of a character unlikely to be encountered in real life. On the imaginal plane, where we meet the flow of meanings and energies between souls and bodies, she and her variants are more feasible.

Kristyn — Steve could see — sucked away meaning, but not like a vampire sucks, because she gained no satisfaction from what she took. What she craved she lacked a place inside herself to keep. Such things can be seen, and their denial is only an equal but opposite exercise of the imagination. What Steve could also see was the underlying principle at work, because there are forces in motion within souls. Love is one of those forces: although there are nothing more various than souls, love is universal, yet channelled in different ways by each. But the force predominant in Kristyn took what she had no capacity to hold, and if it couldn't be hers to process or keep then there was some relationship at least in being its destroyer.

What she sucked inside was made to vanish by this force, for which we have no name except "hatred." But hatred has a limit and often will abate on achieving division from its object. What Steve saw instead is a force with no bounds, endemic, encountered whenever someone attacks another and achieves their aim — yet they persist in attacking. What's gained is never enough, and neither, even, is the opponent's complete obliteration. Where there is no capacity for satisfaction, destruction for destruction's sake is in danger of becoming the sole relationship and aim.

As repugnant as its nature is, Steve recognised this at work in Kristyn, but it wasn't who she was. Hers was a hellish place for anyone to be. He agonised for Bailey most: locked in her orbit and incapable of either escape or approach.

"We should probably make a move, then," Bailey said, sending Steve a look that seemed intended to reassure him he'd done no harm. But Steve knew that whatever was offered to Kristyn she'd destroy, and this put her outside the people in his life he was willing to care about.

"Good to see you," he smiled.

"Probably not really," she said, "but next time, when I'm feeling better."

He was her so-called boyfriend's best friend, and yet she'd asked him nothing, nor expressed any interest, so unbearable for her was giving away attention to anything other than herself.

Turning to Bailey, she said: "You promised to help me move things in the hall."

"What, now?"

"When, then? When am I going to see you again?"

"All right," he sighed.

"Don't worry, you can go out and enjoy yourselves right after."

Stiffly, she pulled herself up. The body beneath her clothes was bony and fragile. She was all bone and grey hair, with a long, pale face, and oversized eyes that glittered bluish grey.

"We won't be long, Steve," said Bailey. "Make yourself comfy."

"Look at some of the books," said Kristyn.

It was a while before they returned. From down the hall he heard irritable conversation, and the sound of things lifted. In his defence — he reflected later — he was doing only what he'd been told. He sat on the sofa, which was warm in an unpleasantly intimate way from Kristyn's body. He flicked through a graphic novel, an intellectual misery memoir that soon bored him. Then his attention fell upon the coloured spines of some notebooks. A green one caught his eye. He reached and opened it.

On the left-hand pages, drawings, with hand-written text on the opposite side. The human figures had no recognisable features. Indeed, their minimalism was extraordinary: in black pencil, so soft the lines were crumbly, the barest marks suggesting the intersection of two bodies. The book was a hand-drawn catalogue of points and modes of contact: lips and genitals; fleshy recesses and tongues; probings of fingers and mouths; gestures of adoration and subjugation. Sexual, but rendered so starkly, so geometrically, that the drawings veered into a vision of eroticism as a tick box list, a series of categorised postures whose meaning was their position in a sequence.

Steve looked through in appalled fascination, conscious this was not something he should see. It was Kristyn and Bailey depicted here, without doubt, but if — as seemed obvious — Kristyn would not have wanted him or anyone to look at this, then it begged the question why she'd taken such meticulous effort to create this visible taxonomy of hers and Bailey's most intimate ... "transactions" was the word that came to mind. It was a ledger, as the text on the facing pages compounded, because against each illustration she'd written a matter-of-fact observation on what had been done and said.

It was nothing that Steve would ever have wanted to know about Bailey, and far less to have seen, not because of what it revealed but, rather, because it provoked his pity. Nowhere in what she'd written had Kristyn mentioned herself — what she'd done, or said, with no indication at all of what she'd wanted. By erasing herself she'd found a means of itemising and objectifying intimacy, as if it were a list of services rendered or injuries endured — a record of reasons why Bailey was in her debt.

Steve put back the notebook and arranged himself for Bailey and Kristyn's imminent return. The drawings, he reasoned, were Kristyn's means of making concrete why she felt Bailey owed her. She hadn't made them for any erotic purpose. He guessed she never intended to show the notebook to Bailey, not even to taunt or pressure him. Rather, her artwork was a binding spell. Crafting those drawings and words had concretised she and Bailey. It conveyed her secret relationship to their relationship, which, having gained its depiction, albeit secret, could now exert a subtle but real effect on their lives. Maybe, thought Steve, it wasn't black magic in the sense of consciously intended malevolence, but only, like any human soul, Kristyn doing what she needed to cope. Yet now he'd seen it, he would have to decide whether to tell Bailey.

Perhaps she had done so once, but currently she wasn't making Bailey happy. Steve's discovery might lend Bailey the impetus he lacked to break loose, and, in the long run, he might even thank Steve for it. Or, just as possibly, it would ruin their friendship. Shame might interpose if it seemed to Bailey that Steve had uncovered what Bailey couldn't. Steve wouldn't be the first to unveil before a couple what ought to have ended them, only to find that instead of turning away from each other they turned on him.

Besides, Bailey didn't need sight of the notebook to work out what was wrong — he was living it, like someone diving into water who knows it's deep and risky, and then he's caught in fronds growing from the bottom, tangled and helpless, fearing for his life, until — with luck more than skill — he escapes. But, although his companions disclose later they knew that at the bottom there were weeds, on returning to the surface and relating his ordeal, he holds them blameless: he knew the risk when he dived in, and even having known what his friends omitted to mention, it would have been no guarantee of safety. This was what Steve reasoned: it didn't matter what he, Steve, knew, because the obligation was on Bailey to handle it.

When Bailey and Kristyn returned, Steve pretended to read the boring novel he'd put down long before. It wasn't hard to act as if nothing had happened, because nothing that made a difference had. It might feel as if knowing about someone's sex life means something important, but sex — like love, or even like that nameless destruction he'd seen in Kristyn — is only yet another force that works impersonally. If through every river in the world water flows, then what's revealed about rivers by water? The notebook exposed Bailey's sex-life, his desire, but where were the surprises? Desire is simple. The notebook said more about Kristyn than Bailey, because pushing away, deflection, demands more effort than desire and, for that reason, exposes more. It's the twists and turns, the defiles and obstacles that reveal and define the river, rather than the simple fact that it contains water.

So, yes, there were things he and Bailey had never shared, because with the perspective that magick offers onto another world comes an understanding that many of the things in this one are more of the same. The writings in the notebook may indeed have depicted Bailey's sexual repertoire: things he did, or liked to do; words he uttered in passion. But he was just as much a mystery to Steve as ever, because the real question wasn't what Bailey's relationship to Kristyn was like, but why. Steve had imagined himself and Bailey in similar terms, like spaceships in orbit. Donna as a planet, or a world. Woman as earth or matter, as territory. This was imagery with an ancient provenance. If Kristyn were a black hole, that too was a metaphor unshy of stereotypes. Yet the issue was not the nature of women but the enigma of Bailey's attraction to Kristyn, because although it was wonderful to visit other worlds, no good could come from proximity to a black hole. Past the event horizon is no prospect of return. The best that can ever be hoped for is a stable orbit, but this poses the hazard of never breaking loose. And there — thought Steve — was maybe, for Bailey, the source of the allure.

anabasis

"War seems inevitable," said Bailey. "It feels different now, though, doesn't it? Back in the day, it felt as if conflict would break out accidentally. But today, no — it will definitely be deliberate. People are talking about limited nuclear exchanges, as if that were thinkable. It's like we're being groomed for a world in which this is accepted."

"To think it's allowable, you've got to be asleep," agreed Steve. "Oblivious to being a living, mortal creature."

"You can be conscious of a feeling that you're not alive," said Bailey. "When you consider it, that reveals everything about what being human means."

"It always feels like the present is different from the past, and that we can escape the past," said Steve. "But then the past comes around again, and it's evident once more that — like war — it's only possible to forget it for a while. Everything avoided or denied, it's all still there. This really is the world of the dead, but the living imagine it's theirs."

Dinner was over and they were drinking wine in the lounge. Music played. Donna was clearing up in the kitchen. She didn't need to. Steve had noticed how she'd been up and down, in and out of the room ever since Bailey arrived, obsessing more than usual.

"What will it be like when bombs are dropping here again?" Steve wondered.

"Different from the last time," said Bailey. "It'll need to be. There's no way they could sell conscription to people these days. Who would go die in a ditch for a politician?"

"Will it be different, though? Isn't this forgetting again what always happened in the past?"

"It's corrupt," said Bailey. "And I don't mean people, but all the way down into reality itself. This ought to lead us in a certain direction, otherwise nothing makes sense and existence seems a kind of torture."

"That's why the dead were pissed off," said Steve.

"*The dead came back from Jerusalem*," quoted Bailey, "*where they found not what they sought*. Are they angry because we've not worked it out?"

"Jerusalem, most likely, is where it'll all kick off," said Steve. "What lessons can we teach the dead?"

It may seem presumptuous to suppose that an undistinguished life produces wisdom that might benefit the dead, and yet the vastest lessons inhabit the homeliest remarks. Sometimes they issue from relatives, or chance encounters. Steve remembered chatting with an old guy on a bus, travelling back from an interview where he'd failed to land the job he really needed. "Well," smiled the old guy, "if they don't want you then they won't have you." It had wounded Steve, because he supposed the old guy was saying he was unlikeable, but his eyes were shining. Then the meaning of it clicked, and Steve beamed gratefully at the old guy, released from the feeling of failure, because — as he'd stated so succinctly — the outcome, despite Steve's efforts, wasn't his to control. Whether or not it was intended, what the old guy said had been a lesson in non-attachment deeper than any Buddhist *sutta*.

The deepest conversations are between lovers, strangers, and friends. The bigger the truth, the closer to home it's found, and the biggest truth is invisible, because it's nearer than near.

Whereas the dead have only a power to question or demand, the living have agency to muster a response, a potential answer, albeit insufficient or wrong. It's not knowledge that helps the dead but proximity. Reticence, from fear of ignorance, creates only an unconstructive distance.

"Back to what you were saying at dinner," said Steve, "about the descent demanding renunciation of any intention to return, and the recognition that this world is the underworld, contrary to appearance ...."

"It's what she showed me," said Bailey.

"The problem," said Steve, "is then there's no difference between the shades and us."

"Well, if you know better then tell me," said Bailey, "because you've been hanging out with them."

"No, you tell me," said Steve. "I've come to know the dead, but I'm not in their world. You say that you are, and that you're never coming out."

I fear for Hugin, that he come not back, thought Bailey.

"Isn't this Theseus and Pirithous?" said Steve.

Bailey's eyes widened for a second, and then he nodded. Yes. Theseus and Pirithous: friends who'd descended into the underworld together. Both of their wives had died, and so — as a means, perhaps, to safeguard against future repetition of loss — they'd pledged to marry each a daughter of Zeus. Theseus chose Helen of Sparta — who would be known, later, more famously, as Helen of Troy. At this time, she was barely a teen, so, having whisked her away, they lodged her safely until she came of age with Theseus's mum. Meanwhile, Pirithous set his sights on an even higher prize: the goddess herself. His plan: to snatch her from her husband, Hades, and then, doubly abducted, she would be his bride back home in Thessaly.

Theseus tried to talk some sense into him, but Pirithous couldn't see the audacity of his intention. Bad enough that reality had needed to be reconfigured when first of all Hades had taken the goddess away, but now Pirithous was idiot enough to picture doing it over again. Theseus understood the goddess was out of their league but, bound by his pledge, assented to aid his friend. So down they went, and down and down, until, wearied by the descent, they sat on rocks to rest a moment, and then — horrified — discovered themselves superglued to their seats and utterly incapable of rising. Evidently, Zeus was one step ahead of them.

But, as luck would have it, on an unrelated mission the doughty hero Herakles was passing by. He lifted Theseus from the rock, but when he made to extend the same to Pirithous, the earth shook with divine rage. So, Pirithous stayed stuck to his rock in the underworld, and bade farewell forever to his friend. This was Pirithous's fate for his role in that ill-judged heist.

"It's always the tiny details where you find the meat."

"It is," said Steve. "Due to having parts in bigger stories, both the women they chose were unavailable."

"That's where Pirithous went wrong," said Bailey. "You can devote yourself to her, or be taught by her, but you don't marry a goddess."

"If what Theseus did had happened a few years later, he might've started the Trojan war. He opted for a prize that could only be enjoyed in years to come. The mistake of Pirithous, apart from hubris, was to decide on a goal that could never be realised."

"I can see what you're doing," smiled Bailey. "Because this is the underworld, and we can never emerge from it, you think I've renounced life."

"Whoever chooses the goddess of the underworld remains there with her, surely?" laughed Steve.

"We die to the world, and to our delusion of possessing the goddess," said Bailey. "Pirithous didn't realise that. Even if he had, that's not the same as giving up on life."

"He set his sights on someone it was impossible to be with," said Steve.

"But really," countered Bailey, "Theseus went wrong too. The Helen he abducted was the girl, not the woman. He never knew nor appreciated who she really was."

"He knew she was a daughter of Zeus," said Steve.

"Anyhow, there's another detail," said Bailey. "While he and Pirithous were stuck down there, wondering how to get out, Helen's brothers, the Dioscuri — you know, the twins in Gemini — they went and fetched her back from Theseus's mum."

"For Paris to abduct a few years later."

"Yes. Fulfilling her destiny — which she couldn't have done with Theseus, who lost her anyway, because he was on a fool's errand into the land of the dead."

"Theseus stood a chance," said Steve. "Pirithous never did, and should've known it."

Clearly, thought Bailey, Donna had not told Steve about their meeting. Of course, nothing had happened, and neither had he wanted it to. Not particularly. But ever since, he'd been thinking about Donna in a different way. He'd thought about her quite a lot, although maybe it was just more than never, so it had felt like a lot. He had no sensation of sexual desire, nor any intention, but there was a thought, an idea, and he'd taken no action, made no moves, yet it was impossible to deny a feeling that nevertheless he'd crossed a line.

The presence of a thought sends ripples of causation through the world, but what he was feeling did not amount to that, perhaps, nor even to a fantasy of something he could state he wanted. It was even slighter: way down in that register of phantom feelings, a feeling about a feeling. But it was there, and sufficient — as were, he supposed, inclinations even more intangible — to produce certain kinds of changes. Only, he mused, maybe even the notion of "intangible" is illusory. It could be said that the primary axiom of magick is that what's described as imaginary is real, and, if so, there's no denying that whatever is imagined has consequences.

Tiny things producing effects, such as eye contact, which the feeling of his possible feelings made difficult with Donna. Awkwardness between them was nothing new, yet a difference was apparent. Before, looking into one another's eyes was stymied by neither possessing a sense strong enough of at whom they were looking. Now, it was complicated by an impression that looking might reveal what neither wanted to see.

Bailey knew this was the reason that Donna, all evening, had been in and out of the room, never settling long enough to allow this filament of tension to attract Steve's notice. By ducking behind the persona of hostess she'd maintained a workable distance. But Bailey liked it that he'd affected her. If she were reacting to him differently, this affirmed that something had really happened on the day when synchronicity had cast her in the role of goddess. He'd expected she would minimise it. But if she'd chosen to fool herself, then encountering this change it had wrought in him would have elicited nothing from her. Evidently it had, and here they were, living the consequences.

Having caught up with Steve properly, Donna's concerns seemed to Bailey unfounded. Steve had a way of fastening onto things. He did it with people and ideas, and even with things or persons he disliked. Before ever he decided to spit something out, Steve tasted it fully.

He had come through their joint magical working mostly intact, but Bailey thought he detected a sourness in Steve. Magick can produce such states, especially when transacting with the dead because of their incapacity to present any novelty. Interaction can be beneficial, but too much time among the dead turns a magician jaded. These feelings, these states, were a shadow of what Bailey had encountered with the goddess: the state of all experiences becoming equal. Whereas the former concerned the contents of experience (which indeed is tiresome if everything within it is the same), the latter entailed an awareness extended, wherein a thing was as different from everything else as ever, but the moment in which it was arising became the same as any other.

Steve was neither trapped nor isolated. He wasn't drifting away from the living, no matter what Donna thought. How good it must be, thought Bailey, for Steve to have by his side a woman like Donna, so rooted in the world, and yet — as the ravens had revealed — open to other worlds. How impossible it would be then to doubt that the goddess were in the world and metaphysical summer were come.

Pirithous never stood a chance, Steve had said. And he should've known it.

In the town where Bailey and Steve grew up, right against the churchyard gate, was the headstone of a girl who died, aged twelve, in 1849. Hephzibah Ward was her name, which maybe everyone in the town would recognise, because hers was the first stone seen on entering the churchyard. For Bailey, in childhood, her name had symbolised mortality. Hephzibah, no doubt, had hopes and dreams that — dead at twelve — had never stood a chance. None of us stands a chance, thought Bailey. There's only discrepancy between the life that's given, and the one hoped for. Whether or not it's recognised, every tombstone tells the same story. Pirithous and Hephizabah: they couldn't be more dissimilar, nor more alike.

"I'm going to see if Donna wants any help," said Bailey.

"You're a guest," protested Steve.

"No, I want to," said Bailey.

Donna was tidying cupboards in the kitchen. Since moving in, she'd been meaning to do this. She heard Bailey come in, but didn't turn. She'd known that at some point he'd do this. It was obvious from the way he'd been looking at her, and his moody silence. She'd bustled about all evening to signal this wasn't a conversation she needed. But that wasn't the message he wanted, so the signal hadn't been read. The loudness of an intention inside a guy's head drowns out everything. While he's caught in the feeling that there's something he must do, he's oblivious, yet broadcasting exactly what he's about to enact. Only what might happen next matters to him, whereas if he paid attention to the effect his intentions were having already, he would read, plainly, their inevitable outcome.

"Anything I can do to help?" said Bailey.

"No, it's fine," Donna said. "Go and make yourself comfy."

"You're sure? It's been lovely, this evening," said Bailey. "How have you been since our meeting?"

"Better, thanks. What about you? How's Kristyn?"

"Not too bad," said Bailey.

The mention of Kristyn surprised him. He supposed that Steve must've told Donna about that disastrous visit. His face reddened, imagining what Steve had described.

No one is perfect, yet too many people are haunted by a feeling they're not a good person. Suppose, however, that somehow it were revealed it was indeed true. After that, a refusal to change would be a choice to remain not good. He didn't accept that Kristyn was like that; she wasn't willingly bad. She didn't consciously act how she was, yet maybe it was true she resisted — not change, exactly, but perhaps the kind of realisations that would induce it.

People can do strange things with love. Some will throw it right back and hurt the person they received it from, or use it to create distance and hide inside it. There are many couples, who neither like nor love each other, where something similar has happened. Once, there may have been love, but it has been used for something else: as fuel for anger and resentment, or maybe for shame. It's so sad and so strange that this would be chosen over love, but understandable, at least, when the one rejecting love feels that only hatred is what they deserve.

Bailey realised he was exhausted. Weary of being a target for hatred, and of becoming himself a centre of resentment. Being with Kristyn was lonely. It was a form of separation; not a relationship, but only co-existence in the same space.

"I wanted to say," said Bailey, "that Steve's a moron for making you feel lonely. If he would rather cling to the past than reach out for you, then he's an idiot."

Donna stood silently. Bailey took this as an invitation to proceed.

"Steve doesn't see what he has in you, and I didn't either until our meeting. You're incredible, Donna, and no one should make you feel otherwise."

He'd spoken with good intention, but what Donna heard was Bailey's neediness, a craving that extended so deeply he was oblivious to the measly appeal he'd made, for preference over Steve, who Donna had chosen, and who was, supposedly, his best friend.

"I can see that you wanted to say a nice thing," said Donna, "but maybe there're things closer to home you need to work out."

"Hey," said Steve just then, from the kitchen doorway where he'd been listening. "You know I can hear you? What's this about?"

Bailey was glad that Steve had heard. He felt hurt by Donna's rejection. "So why did you come to me for help?" he asked her. But he was talking blindly now, out of pain. He knew she hadn't told Steve about the visit, yet he couldn't see what was clear to Donna: that he'd just now tried to appeal to her over Steve, and now he was appealing to Steve over her. He couldn't do both. It made no sense.

"You two met up without me?" said Steve.

"She asked me to. She was worried," Bailey said.

"Well, okay. I suppose," said Steve, taking it in. He looked at Donna. "It was only a conversation, right?"

"Oh, for god's sake, Steve!" said Donna.

There's a level of need that's ever-present, but it runs so deep it's remote from awareness. It's a level of want so basic that desires closer to the surface become symbols for it; desires such as sex, which seems fundamental. Bailey was reacting from this deeper level, the reason why what he said and did was making no sense. His ham-fisted overtures to Donna were motivated not by sex, regardless how it seemed to him. Donna sensed this. She saw how it came from another place. Not sex, but that underlying craving for wholeness without a name, nor a discernible object, which is why, in desperation, objects are created for it from other urges, to stand in for a lack that nothing fills, because what might fill it is only that which no one can own.

"I met with him because he knows you and the things you do together."

"It's a bit odd that you didn't tell me."

"That was Donna's decision," said Bailey.

"What's going on with you?" Donna turned to Bailey. "You've forgotten that's Steve over there" — she pointed — "He's your best mate. And I'm Donna" — she pointed at herself — "Steve's girlfriend."

"All right," sighed Bailey.

"Is it, though?" said Donna. "Look at where you've both ended up, having done whatever it was that you were doing. Is it really all right?"

I fear for Hugin, that he come not back, thought Bailey. *Yet more anxious am I for Munin.*

During a confrontation, feelings of unreality can enter, as if a dome of glass had descended; everything's visible, but there's a detachment, which — if it's a confrontation over something vital — seems like the least useful thing. He heard what Donna and Steve were saying but could no longer feel it, and it would've been simplest to assume that this was dissociation, triggered by the hurtful truths Donna had voiced, except that Bailey had a strong impression that Donna and Steve felt it too, the same lack of reality.

"Why are we doing this?" he said.

"Why are we?" said Donna, as if someone knew the answer.

"It doesn't feel real, does it?"

"What are you trying to make happen?" Donna said.

"He's stuck on a rock in the underworld," said Steve. "He wants to get off, but can't."

"Yes. I need to get free," said Bailey, feeling a glimmer of reality.

"You can be free because you're not a shade," said Steve.

"We're not like the dead, then?"

"They're not alive. That's all," said Steve. "It took some time, but I've worked out that they're angry because we've forgotten the difference. We judge them by the standards of the present, but their responsibility was to the past. We scapegoat them to avoid our own delusions. They have no case to answer."

"This means you're finished with them, then?" said Donna. "Your mum and dad? Please tell me yes."

"Mum and Dad are gone," nodded Steve. "I can only go back to how they were, and if I find them where they are now, it's different. The life they had is gone. They're dead."

There was a silence, and as they waited for where the conversation would turn, the secretive sound of the kitchen light became audible, a faint, dry humming that betrayed the illusion of continual light — a subtle sound of flickering on and off, so high and fast it seemed illumination was never absent, whereas, in fact, it depended upon pulsation: light interrupted by intervals of dark. The alternation wasn't visible, except, by concentrating hard, the fluctuation could be sensed as a paradoxical impression of darkness wrapped in light, like something dry and bitter which at the same time was quenching and sweet.

Everything flickers. Between each fervent burst nothingness persists and, under the kitchen light in that room, or wherever else they went, the dead would always be there.

"How do I get out?" asked Bailey.

Steve sighed and motioned at Bailey and Donna to come into the lounge and sit. Then he told them both about the green notebook he'd found on Kristyn's shelf, and what she'd drawn and written.

When Herakles went down to bust loose Theseus and Pirithous from the rocks onto which Hades had superglued them, he didn't succeed at setting Pirithous free. Theseus escaped, barely — literally, by the skin of his arse, according to those tellings that relate how a portion of his buttocks remained stuck to the rock. (*Hypolispos* he was known as. "Smooth arse.") Herakles was sent to save them, but a better approach than wrenching Pirithous bodily off the rock would've been to provide him with his own means of removal. The one sure way to gain an exit from the underworld — minus a saviour — is self-disqualification from its torments, rearrangement of attitude and situation, such that what's received there is no longer either invited nor deserved. This is the golden key to the gates of hell, which — to confirm a pervasive rumour — are locked from the inside.

It's more than a rumour, maybe. When created by bad choices, then hell and its sufferings offer a refuge in what's personal and familiar. It's not nice in there, but then it never has been, and from its recognisability comes the feeling of a home. The underworld offers a negative paradise, and it was for this reason that Bailey, rather than upset or angry, above all else was bewildered when Steve disclosed — with details so personal to Bailey that Steve couldn't have known them unless it were true — how Kristyn had desecrated the very little that still remained between them.

Bailey understood how it never had been the case that the relationship didn't work; it served for Kristyn exactly what she intended: safety in rejecting it; the surety that even if she destroyed him, Bailey wouldn't leave. Kidding himself that there was something he could surmount had concealed his own complicity in the binding spell. Desiring the unobtainable — or, rather, pretending to — he'd created this refuge in suffering, a negative paradise, where he'd locked the doors from inside and excused himself from actuality.

Steve's revelation of the notebook blew the gates off from outside and presented the exit. The world was all before him. But Steve was careful — and Donna too, despite the discovery being news to her entirely — to refrain from playing the role of the angel with a flaming sword. Steve reported simply what he'd seen; no negative words towards Kristyn crossed his lips. If Bailey chose to take the exit, then it would be his own decision to renounce the irresponsibility of desiring the unobtainable, the fatal misstep that imprisoned Pirithous for eternity.

"What am I supposed to do with this?"

"You don't have to do anything," said Steve.

"Betrayal is horrible," said Donna.

"There's nothing to be embarrassed at," said Steve.

"Nothing has changed. We're your friends," said Donna.

"Probably there's nothing in her drawings you haven't done with each other," said Bailey.

"That's the thing," Donna said. "It's what the stuff we do means. Outside of a relationship, none of it's special, and that's what she reduced it to."

"I wish I could just stop," sighed Bailey.

"Always, the deeper we go," said Steve, "the bigger the idiocy we discover we've built our lives upon."

"Please, god, I hope that's it for now," Bailey said.

Despite his enduring concern, Odin's ravens were safely home. They'd made their successful circuit of the world. The message from the dead had been deciphered — which hadn't assuaged their rage, but it was heard and understood. The goddess permeated all of it, with her ordeal of dying before death into the underworld and its mysteries. But a final piece, perhaps, had been overlooked.

Donna, implicated in the outcome of Steve and Bailey's magick, hadn't in that countryside layby consented to enter transpersonal realms. That day had been Donna's abduction into an underworld, the kingdom of the dead. Initially, she might not have thanked Steve for sending her there, and for obliging her to contemplate how or whether she must begin to navigate these zones, and yet she'd stayed by his side and had paid no heed to Bailey's inept enticements to believe that Steve didn't see or truly know her.

Forever in the interests of obtaining meaning, of retrieving from the quotidian its mythical core, it can be supposed that the goddess returns to her mother, the earth, for merely a temporary season but with sound motives, and that she feels a belonging equally in the worlds above and below, and that despite his having torn her away from all that was familiar, she was forever in love with Hades. The essence of her power, as queen of the dead, resided in the understanding she possessed, a comprehension unsurpassed, that, beyond identity, the nature of being is permanent displacement, and that her home is a ceaseless transition between disparate realms.

And she hasted and revealed to the doom-giving kings the function of her rites, and enjoined on all her august mysteries, which none may violate or search into or expound, since a great curse from the gods checks the voice. Happy that earth-born man who hath beheld them! He who is not initiate and hath no part therein, never hath equal lot even when dead beneath the mouldy darkness.

— The Homeric Hymns.

about the author

Duncan Barford is a writer and podcaster exploring the intersections between magick, spirituality, psychology, and the paranormal. His previous publications include *Occult Experiments in the Home*, *The Magick of a Dark Song*, and (with Alan Chapman) *The Baptist's Head Compendium*. He lives and works as a psychodynamic counsellor in Sussex, UK.

about sphinx

Sphinx is an imprint of Sul Books. Born from a collaboration of two long-time independent esoteric publishers, and named to honor the Suleviae — the sisterhood of goddesses revered at springs throughout Europe — Sul Books is dedicated to publishing works that manifest aspects of the sacred sight that heals what humans have harmed.

As with the thrice-fold kinship of the Suleviae goddesses, Sul Books combines the publishing strength of three resilient imprints: Sphinx Books, RITONA, and Gods&Radicals Press. Arising from these continuing legacies comes a fourth, committed to stand-out works of powerful transformation.

Find our other titles at Sulbooks.com

www.ingramcontent.com/pod-product-compliance
Lightning Source LLC
Chambersburg PA
CBHW032012180726
48283CB00008B/2648